Texas Winter

RJ Scott

Texas Winter

Texas series, book 2
Copyright ©2016 RJ Scott
Smashwords Edition
Cover design by Meredith Russell
Edited by Sue Adams

Published by Love Lane Books Limited
ISBN 978-1484096765

Dedication

For all those readers who wanted more Riley and Jack.
And, as always, for my family.

CHAPTER 1

"Phone," Jack mumbled.

Blindly reaching past Riley and fumbling for the offending item, he managed to grab it and check who was calling: Unknown Number. Irritation shot through him, but he wasn't sure if it was at the offending caller or because Riley's phone wasn't on silent for their precious two hours of sleep. He could just imagine it was a freaking reporter, still after interviews even after all this time. A whole year had passed since Jeff's shooting, yet the tabloid press remained hungry for Campbell-Hayes stories.

"What?" Riley was about as lucid as Jack, and he raised his head, eyes half-open.

His blond hair was sleep mussed and probably—Jack considered—sex mussed. His hazel eyes looked bloodshot, and in that second it wasn't irritation Jack felt for Riley at his inability to turn off his cell, but affection and love. "Go back to sleep," he ordered.

Riley didn't argue. He lay back down on the pillow and resumed the rhythmic, heavy breathing Jack had gotten used to.

Jack tried to sleep himself, but even though the instant panic he had felt at the call had subsided, his brain refused to stop thinking. Cautiously he edged out of the huge bed and snuck a quick look at the early morning outside their villa.

The Caribbean Sea was a sparkling sapphire blue, and the beach was empty of a single soul.

When Riley had presented Jack with tickets for what he enthusiastically called a honeymoon, Jack had every single excuse under the sun ready to avoid going. The horses needed him; his mom was getting too friendly with the veterinarian; Emily had started to talk, and they didn't want to miss that; Josh was busy with the newest addition to his family—baby Sarah—and couldn't watch the ranch. The Double D needed new fencing, and Jack had to be the one to do the work.

Riley listened to every excuse. In fact, the detailed excuses filled a good ten minutes.

Jack told him it wasn't that he didn't want to go. Hell, the thought of any time alone with Riley sounded good to him. It was just… kicking back and doing nothing? That would be a first for Jack, and the thought of it didn't sit comfortably.

Riley, the bastard, did what he was so good at. He said nothing and simply allowed Jack to get it all off his chest, and then he just looked at Jack with soulful eyes and a pleading expression on his face. "It's only ten days, and I need the time with you."

Such a simple statement, but enough to win Jack over in an instant. The last year had been full of ups and downs, but Jack's worries were small compared to everything Riley had been through: his brother dying, his sister-in-law being responsible for the murder, and his father taking the blame before succumbing to cancer himself. Then there was the whole parentage issue with Beth's baby.

Riley worked hard, and he and Jack played hard, but every so often Riley would get lost in everything that had happened and guilt would trip him up. Added to that,

Riley was hip-deep in working on the auction for exploration rights of millions of acres of undersea minerals in the western Gulf of Mexico. As young as he was, Riley's expertise and his position on the board of Hayes Oil were enough for his fledgling consultancy in ethical exploration for oil to grow exponentially.

There had been too many days apart, and Jack didn't like to think of himself as clingy, but jeez, at least one full weekend together would be good.

"Okay, we'll go," Jack finally agreed.

And thank God he had. Because that meant he was with Riley in this island paradise, and he could slip open the door, step onto the golden sands, and run to the water. Diving into the cerulean sea would be a sudden wake-up call at this time of the morning, but there were only two better ways to wake up, in Jack's opinion—either lying with Riley's arms wrapped around him, or standing at the corral fence, watching the Texas dawn spread over his land.

He unlocked the door and opened it quietly.

"Don't go."

Jack stopped and looked back at the bed where he had left a comatose man, expecting to see his husband awake but sleepy. Instead he got an eyeful of sheets pushed back to reveal six-four of tanned, muscled, naked Riley. Not only that, but Riley's hand curled around a rather impressive morning erection, and he had the biggest, most suggestive grin on his face Jack had seen since yesterday morning's welcoming smile.

"I wanted a swim," Jack mock protested.

"And I want you naked and draped over me."

Riley arched up into his fist, and it was a beautiful sight—his husband naked and ready, acres of warm, toned skin available to touch. "Is *that* supposed to make me stay, Het-boy?" Jack belied the joking words as he locked the door and let the drapes fall back, the room moving from light to dark in an instant. Not dark enough to hide the mouthwatering sight of Riley Campbell-Hayes running his hand up and down his cock and arching into the motion.

Riley reached out with his free hand and grabbed the nearly empty bottle of lube from the bedside cabinet. He aimed and then threw the lube at Jack, who caught it deftly.

"One of us is overdressed." Riley looked pointedly at the shorts Jack had pulled on to go for a swim.

Jack pasted an innocent look on his face and pushed the shorts down his legs until they pooled on the floor. If he took a little extra time to do so, then sue him. Riley wasn't the only one who could tease.

"What do you want me to do with this?" He indicated the lube in his hand, then climbed as gracefully as he could onto the bed and straddled Riley's knees, taking his fill of the striking body laid out under him. From wide shoulders to narrow hips, broad chest to an impressive dick, Riley was perfection personified. Not to mention the slight scattering of dark blond hair on Riley's chest and the dark-tinted nipples waiting to be sucked and bitten.

"It's my turn, cowboy," Riley said, "so I'm guessin' you need to be gettin' some fingers in your ass."

Jack loved it when Riley was so turned on his accent slid from educated city boy to pure Texan cowboy in an instant.

"Your turn, huh?" Jack began seriously.

He opened the lube and poured a more than generous amount onto his fingers. They may have made love last night and into the morning, but shit, Riley's dick was freaking huge, and Jack really needed to make sure he was stretched enough to be comfortable.

"Check the notches on my side of the headboard." Riley arched into his fist and ran his tongue over his bottom lip, leaving a slide of glistening moisture.

It was an invitation Jack couldn't refuse. Despite the hottest sex he had ever experienced in his life with a lover who didn't hold back, it was the intimacy of kissing Jack he ached to share. He leaned down and traced the path of Riley's tongue with his own, pulling at his lower lip with his teeth and then releasing the plump skin.

The kisses deepened, and as they kissed, Jack leaned on one hand and used the other to loosen and lubricate himself. His dick was ready, leaking and so freaking hard. Every so often it brushed Riley's in electric contact.

Riley's hand snaked around Jack, joining Jack's fingers and stretching with him. With the feel of Riley's fingers inside him too and the slickness of the lube, Jack panted his need into Riley's mouth way too soon. He pushed down, then raised himself off, before shuffling higher up the bed and using his lubed hand to line Riley up.

In seconds they were together, Riley buried so far inside him, the shock of being filled dissipating in the desperation of need and want. Jack set the rhythm, leaning in briefly for more kisses and then sitting up. Riley wrapped his hands around Jack's dick and closed his eyes.

The sight and sound of Riley arching and moaning and

pleading was going to send Jack over the edge far too fast, and he couldn't stop.

"Open your eyes," Riley pleaded. All Jack could do was shake his head. "Please, open them. Look at me when we come together."

Jack's orgasm was building, and with thrust after thrust, completion came closer. Riley's hand on his dick became more erratic, a sure sign he was close, and finally, Jack opened his eyes.

Riley's face was flushed red, his eyes wide, his mouth slack, and Jack let himself go. With a final move, a twist and the scrape of Riley's dick over his prostate, he lost it hot and wet over Riley's stomach. The tensing of Riley's muscles sent Jack high, and the feeling of being filled was exquisite.

"I love you, Jack."

"I love you too." Jack pulled off as gently as he could and slid boneless to one side of Riley. "God, I love you."

* * * * *

Laughing like kids, they grabbed swim shorts and suntan lotion ready to set off for the beach. Jack had packed a bag with towels and books and a multitude of other vital beach stuff, and Riley picked up his phone. After a second's consideration, which Jack watched without making it obvious, he simply dropped it in the top drawer. They only had two more days here, and Jack was relieved Riley was finally letting go of the office.

They spent all day at the shoreline, talking, planning and discussing the family.

"He's a nice guy," Riley offered carefully.

Jack shook his head. "He's twenty years younger than Mom." He had the age gap worked out to the nearest day the minute his mom revealed she felt affection for Neil Kendrick, the new veterinarian at the horse practice they used.

"But he makes her happy."

"He's living in a one-room rental."

"He only moved there three months ago. Give him a break."

"He's not what I want for her."

"It's her choice."

"It might be a money thing. Maybe I should get a PI to check him out."

"For God's sake, Jack, you can't get a PI to check out the vet just because your momma is sweet on him."

Jack subsided into silence. He couldn't think of what to say. It wasn't that he didn't want his mom to be happy—he did. Beth and Josh had families, he had Riley, and she had spent so much time being there for her family, she'd left herself on her own. Neil seemed like a nice enough guy, so maybe he should listen to Riley or have a quiet word. Jeez. It was the age gap… that was all.

He looked over at Riley who was face down on the towel. Every second Riley was out here, he lost more of the office pallor he wore so well. He was turning as brown as a nut.

"I'm not saying you're right," Jack offered grudgingly. "He's a nice enough guy, good with the horses. I'll…." When he trailed off, Riley looked up at him expectantly. "I'll try. Okay?"

Riley smiled his approval and then clambered to stand. "I'm hungry." He patted his stomach to emphasize the words.

"You're always hungry," Jack muttered and used Riley's offered hand to stand up.

They hugged quickly, and Jack luxuriated in the expanse of Riley's warm skin. They finally pulled apart to pick up the items they'd brought with them.

"Shower, food, nap, sex." Riley counted off the options in order on his fingers, and slowly, hand in hand, they made their way back to the weathered villa at the tree line.

The shower was heaven. The food was delivered as they dried off, and they consumed it all with uncurbed enthusiasm. The nap was more cuddling and talking than actual sleeping, and only disturbed when Riley's phone sounded again from the drawer.

"I'm expecting a call from Travers and the consortium," Riley explained. With a wryly apologetic expression, he opened the drawer and pulled out his iPhone, glancing down at the screen. He did a double take as he read.

Jack read over his shoulder. "Twelve missed calls and three voice mails? Is this consortium thing a problem for you?"

Riley hadn't said much about the latest consultation he was involved in, apart from the usual. Setting up CH Consultancy had been tough on Riley on top of everything else. He was in the house office one hell of a lot, and his cell phone was his constant companion.

"Not really," Riley answered. "I thought it was done and dusted before we left for here." He thumbed to his voice mail. The list only had one name on it: Eden Hayes.

Riley listened to his voice mails, and Jack watched his reaction for any clues as to what the problem was. Riley just looked more and more confused with every second.

Then he went white. Literally every single element of color left his face and he dropped the cell. It fell to the floor and bounced to a stop next to the mini bar.

"Ri?" Jack asked, shocked.

Riley didn't say a thing—just stared at Jack in utter shock.

"What is it? Talk to me." Still no reply, and Jack was growing more scared. "Is it the family? Eden? Beth's baby? What?"

"It was Eden," Riley finally offered. His voice was dead flat with no emotion. "She's sending the jet. We have to go home."

Riley stood and crossed to the suitcases, opening his and scooping clothes from the closet haphazardly into the space. Jack wasn't sure what to say, but actions spoke louder than words, anyway. He stopped Riley with a firm grip on his muscled arms and pushed himself into Riley's space.

"What's wrong? Tell me what happened."

He shook Riley slightly to snap him out of whatever shock was driving the instinct to pack and not talk.

Riley blinked his way back to the world, and sorrow filled his eyes. It was a heartbreaking expression, and Jack had seen it too many times since meeting Riley not to know something terrible must have happened. He put two and two together and came up with the only solution that would make sense of all this.

"Did they find out about what Lisa did?"

No one outside of a few family members knew it had been Lisa, Jeff's wife, who had shot him, because Riley's father had taken the fall. If anyone found out now, it would mean ruin for far too many people with secrets.

"No. It's me."

"You?"

"God. I'm so sorry. I didn't know."

Riley's face held so much grief.

"Ri, you're scaring me."

"Eden said...." Riley twisted his fingers into his short hair, closing his eyes.

"What!"

"A daughter." Riley opened his eyes, and his expression was anguished. "Fuck, Jack. I have a daughter."

CHAPTER 2

"What?" Jack was shocked, and that was an understatement. He wasn't sure that what he'd heard was what Riley actually said. Maybe he'd heard wrong?

"The calls. All of them. They were from Eden. The child's great-aunt has been trying to contact me through her. Shit, Jack. There's a letter that says I'm the dad."

A dad? Riley couldn't have fathered a kid since they'd married—he hadn't had time to cat around on him.

No. He dismissed the instant reaction with an internal flush of shame. Riley wouldn't do that anyway. They loved each other. "When was the baby born?"

"She's eight," Riley said, much to Jack's relief, and he slumped to the bed, resting his elbows on his knees and putting his head in his hands.

"Okay. So you were what? Twenty?"

"In college. The woman—girl—Lexie, she was in my business course. I remember the name."

Jack bit his tongue trying to follow this line of thought. Given what he knew of Riley's past, even remembering a name at all was an achievement. Riley's time before his marriage had been one long party.

"So you have a letter. That doesn't prove anything. We'll get blood tests. Fight it if you need to."

Riley looked up at him, grim determination bracketing his mouth. "I remember her. Lexie, I mean. She was just someone I hooked up with, but it lasted longer than most, nearly three months. I liked her. Jeez, I even took her home for Easter, introduced her to my family, for what it was worth. She was normal, you know. Not society, not a daughter of someone who thought a lot of themselves. Just a girl I sat next to in business studies." Riley frowned. "She disappeared. Just up and left a few weeks after the break, left some note about moving colleges and thanks, but no thanks."

"She left you when she found out she was pregnant, then?"

"I don't know. The note was brief."

"You didn't suspect she was pregnant?"

Riley shook his head. "No, and I was always so careful. Always."

"Not everything works 100 percent of the time, Ri. You know that." Jack hadn't meant to be so blunt, but he was trying his hardest to find the right thing to say.

"Shit," Riley said miserably.

"Look, she may be testing the waters to see how much money she can get from you, and getting a paternity test is easy. Worst-case scenario, if she's entitled to any of your money for child support, then it can be cleared up one way or the other out of court. Best case, it'll prove you're in the clear."

Riley stared back at him with wide eyes. Laying out the extremes was something Jack felt Riley should hear. He'd expected him to agree, but what Riley said next rocked Jack to the core.

"She's not going to fight it." Riley closed his eyes. "She's dead, Jack. That's why Eden called me. They were at the house. With Lexie's daughter. Her name is Hayley. Funny, that. Hayley Hayes."

Jack dropped to his knees between Riley's legs, looking

up at him. The last part sounded like Riley was close to losing his cool. In his shock, all his words were staccato. "Whatever this is, we can get through it." Unspoken was the "together" he'd left off at the end of the sentence.

"What if she's actually mine? What will I do?"

Riley was looking to Jack for reassurance, for just the right words that would make this all okay. Jack's heart clenched and emotion choked his throat. Inside, he'd always known that one day something from Riley's past would come and kick them both to the curb. Something from his old Hayes Oil days, something about Jeff's death… anything but a freaking child born to an ex.

Still, it didn't change how Jack felt, and his instant reaction was one of "we'll get through this."

"We," he offered simply. He emphasized the single word with a gentle poke to Riley's broad chest. "You mean what will *we* do?"

"I don't…," Riley began and then stopped, unable to meet Jack's gaze.

Jack wasn't going to waste time wondering what space Riley was disappearing into. He needed cold, hard facts to make decisions.

Riley said sadly, "I don't know what's going to happen here. I don't know anything. Eden just said I need to get home."

"Let's go." Jack injected as much encouragement into his voice as he could find.

Leaving Riley sitting in numb, silent shock, Jack began to pack.

* * * * *

The Hayes Oil jet stood stationary at the end of the island's runway. Jack couldn't help but remember another time he had walked to the airplane with a similar shock inside him. That time he had been on his way to an arranged marriage with a man who was blackmailing him. This time he was trying to filter everything dumped onto Riley by a freaking phone call, and it wasn't easy.

Riley was deadly quiet, and Jack didn't know what to say. His husband was lost in thought and looking more and more distressed as time passed. Jack didn't know what would be best thing to do, but he didn't want to lose Riley to memories. Jack made decisions based on evidence, and part of him considered the matter something they couldn't concentrate on until they were aware of all the facts.

They boarded in silence, Riley obviously still deep in thought, and were in the air and on their way back home within ten minutes.

"Shit," Riley swore as he undid his seat belt and started pacing the stark interior of the jet.

Jack removed his own belt and leaned forward in his seat. He waited. Riley had every right to get everything out of his system, and as much as Jack wanted to prevent him from losing it, he stopped himself from interfering. Jack expected more swearing and blustering, and completely blown away when all Riley did was slump down in the seat opposite his and bury his head in his hands.

"I'm really sorry."

Riley's emotions were so close to the surface, Jack could feel every single one of them. "Stop apologizing," he ordered. He hated it when Riley felt like he needed to keep saying sorry.

"Sorry," Riley instantly said again, and then he smiled briefly at his reaction. "Okay, I won't do any more apologizing." Then he sat upright and stared straight at Jack.

"How are you feeling?" Jack asked. Whether his husband would be able to vocalize how he was feeling was another matter altogether. Riley Campbell-Hayes was good at the art of saying nothing and internalizing everything.

After a brief pause, Riley answered. "Pissed. Sad. Scared."

Well, that was a start, Jack thought. Riley appeared to have experienced most of the natural emotions after a shock in one hit. "We need to talk."

Riley leaned forward and looked more serious and earnest than Jack had ever seen him. "I've been thinking, just from the instant reaction of it all. It's way more than you signed on for. If she's mine, if she's a Hayes, or hell, even if she isn't mine, but she's alone? I couldn't turn her away."

"I know you couldn't, Ri." Compassion filled Jack as he saw the decisions flying across Riley's expression. His husband could no more turn away a child than Jack could.

"So what I wanted to say is…." Riley sighed and reached for Jack's hand, gripped it tightly. "I won't hold you to anything. And I would understand if you decided an instant child, a daughter, was too much."

The words came out in a rush of emotion, and it took a few seconds for Jack to filter through the meaning of what

Riley was saying. When he did finally understand, Jack didn't know how he felt the most—pissed that Riley thought Jack would back off, or proud that Riley wasn't questioning the child's place somewhere in his own life. Pride won, along with a healthy dose of affection.

"Okay," Jack said carefully. He mimicked Riley's stance and leaned forward. "Come closer so I can hit you for being stupid. Do you think that would help?"

"Hit me?" Shock appeared to push through the glassy-eyed sincerity Riley had been trying for. He glanced down to where Jack's hands rested on the arms of the seat and then back up at Jack's face. This time his expression held uncertainty.

"I'm going to say this once," Jack said carefully. "You are my husband, and what happens to you happens to me. Does that make it clear?"

Riley nodded. "It does. I'm just so tired."

"We haven't slept for a while. We're gonna need clear heads back home, so maybe we should try and get some rest now?"

"I don't think I can."

Riley held himself stiffly as Jack tugged on his hand and led him to the couch at the back of the jet. It was dark and soft and incredibly comfortable, and stood dead opposite a huge flat-screen TV. Jack flicked to a music channel, and they sat side by side. Within minutes, Riley was leaning against Jack, his eyes closed in slumber.

Jack didn't join him in sleep for a while. His brain was as full as it had been this morning. This time, though, there was a fresh worry inside him and a new space for contemplation. He hadn't been joking when he'd said he could have smacked Riley for thinking he'd back away at the first sign of trouble. Right now he chalked it up to shock and thought little more on the matter.

Instead he concentrated on the little girl who'd been brought to Dallas, looking for a daddy.

Children were something dancing around the edges of Jack's life plans. To maybe adopt and to extend his family with Riley was one part of his future. He hadn't taken the thoughts any further, including not mentioning them to Riley.

Hayley might well be a destined part of their family. It wouldn't be easy taking on an eight-year-old whose momma had just died. She was currently being taken care of by a great-aunt. Jack's heart ached for the little girl and her big world of scary monsters.

Riley interrupted his thoughts by murmuring in his sleep. Jack strained to listen but couldn't make out the restless words. Compassion welled inside him because he felt sure Riley's dreams were not good ones. Wondering whether he should wake him up, Jack rested a hand on Riley's arm, but instead of shaking him awake, he smoothed his hand up and down Riley's taut muscles, in a rhythmic motion. He didn't stop until Riley turned closer and buried his face in the juncture of Jack's neck and shoulder.

Shifting slightly, Jack allowed himself to sink lower in the sofa. Riley naturally curled into him and followed the movement. Lulled by Riley's rhythmic breathing and the huff of each breath warm on his neck, it didn't take Jack long to follow him into sleep.

CHAPTER 3

The plane touched down early in the evening and taxied to the private area at Love Field. Jack woke Riley, and they were ready to disembark as soon as the door opened. The steps to the tarmac were steep, and Jack was so lost in thought, he wasn't concentrating. He stumbled a few steps down from the top, only stopping himself from tumbling to the ground by grabbing Riley. They stopped. Jack because his heart was suddenly racing with adrenaline, and Riley because Jack had his arm in a grip so tight he knew there would be bruises.

"You okay?" Riley looked worried and glanced from Jack's hand to his face and back again.

Jack didn't release the grip. Suddenly it hit him that when their feet hit Texas soil, nothing would ever be the same again. Whether they were dads to Hayley or not, a very different path had been chosen for them. They were no longer just a couple.

He needed to tell Riley everything spinning in his head. Things like: Riley shouldn't worry about what was happening, Jack would stay with him whatever happened, and he was excited at the idea of meeting a little-girl version of Riley.

He raised a free hand and traced Riley's angular face, settling the fingers into his short blond hair and staring deep into hazel eyes that looked greener today. Love and lust and need clutched at him, and he wondered, not for the first time, if he would ever get enough of this man. "I love you," he offered gently.

Riley's concerned expression relaxed at the simple words, and he smiled. They met in the middle and sealed the private moment with a gentle kiss before Jack let go of Riley's arm and they continued down to the airstrip.

Their luggage sat in a small pile, and each picked up a large bag and a case. There really was nothing Riley or Jack could do about Hayley until morning, and home was where they needed to be right then. They passed through customs, and Eden was waiting in the private parking for the VIP landing zone.

With little ceremony, they placed their bags in the trunk. Riley pulled his sister close for a hug, and they held each other for a long time. Jack was relieved he'd done that rather than launch into a thousand and one questions. However, it all changed as soon as Riley climbed into the shotgun seat, confining Jack to the back seat.

Riley addressed Eden. "What else can you tell me? Tell us?"

Jack noticed the correction and met Riley's gaze in the mirror with an encouraging smile.

"It started two days ago. I tried not to phone you before I needed to," she began as she pulled out of the main gate and headed east. "We had a visit from this woman in her seventies, toting along a little girl. Said the child's mother was a woman called Lexie Samuels—and she was Lexie's great-aunt— and she was looking for Riley Nathaniel Hayes. She had a letter that her niece gave her, naming you as the father of the child, together with a whole bundle of paperwork. She said she was coming back tomorrow at nine, and there needed to be something in place for the child. Then she said, right in front of the little girl, that the child needed a placement fast because her mom had just died."

"What kind of person does that?" Jack commented.

"She seemed distraught. I'm not sure she was thinking."

"Still, does she even have a freaking heart?"

"She was exhausted, and she looked ill. She'd tracked you to the Hayes house. The new owners said we'd gone and sent her to the D. Donna called me, and I got there as soon as I could. We asked them to stay."

"At the D?" Jack asked.

"Yeah, but she said no. Said Hayley wasn't staying until she'd spoken to Riley."

"So, what happened? Did she take the child somewhere else? To a hotel? Is she okay? Do you know where they went?"

Riley's questions tumbled haphazardly out of him. Eden held up a hand to quiet her brother. She could stop him talking with that single action as effectively as Jack could with two ropes and a jar of lube.

"They went to the Oak. They'd been dropped off at the D by cab, so I drove them to the motel."

"Do you think she's mine?"

"Hell, Riley, there's no doubt she's yours. She looks just like me when I was her age. She has our hair, our eyes. I don't for one minute think she is anyone else's *but* yours."

They reached the outskirts of Dallas, heading for open country, and she stepped on the gas as they moved onto clearer roads.

"Lexie was my girlfriend," Riley said wistfully. "Eden,

do you remember I brought her home?"

Eden shook her head and punctuated the action with a huge sigh. "To be honest, Ri, I don't remember her. But I'm surprised this hasn't happened before. Considering the amount of girls you went through then and since, you're lucky you're not the father of twelve."

Eden wasn't laughing; she was deadly serious. Riley didn't rise to the sibling censure, but it made Jack wince.

"Has the press gotten involved yet?" Jack was just being pragmatic. It was Riley and Eden's reality. The press followed the Hayes family like vultures.

"Not so far. She didn't mention taking the story to the press, and there was no threat in her visit. She was just resigned. But we should think about keeping it quiet. Whatever the outcome." Eden's voice was firm.

Jack wanted to defuse the tension in the car, but mostly he wanted to see the soft-hearted side of Eden rather than this practical woman. "Eden, can you tell us about her?"

She was quick to answer, and this time there was affection in her voice. "Small. Itty-bitty girl with blonde hair to her waist and huge brown eyes. Very quiet. She didn't say anything, just looked at me and the ranch and the horses and then hid her face."

"I don't understand. Why'd the great-aunt bring her to the D? Poor kid just lost her momma." Jack made the question sound more like an observation and qualified it with his reasoning. "Surely she could have waited to be sure Riley was there."

"Apparently the girl asked her great-aunt to find your family quickly."

"She asked her that?" Riley looked sharply at his sister.

"Wanted to meet her daddy, she said."

And with that statement Jack knew it wouldn't matter if Hayley had Hayes blood or not. She was theirs.

They were going to be daddies.

* * * * *

The ranch didn't look any different from when they'd left. The road was as pitted, the fence as pristine, and the horses turned out in the paddocks and acreage of the Double D.

Donna was waiting for them at the main house, eager to hand out hugs to them. In fact, Jack felt like they'd never left.

"I have coffee," his momma said simply. "And cookies."

Typically, his mom was dealing with a crisis by using a combination of caffeine and chocolate and her patented hugs.

Seated at the scarred kitchen table, they spoke very little about the elephant in the room to start with, and no one asked the question that really needed an answer. No one said "what are you going to do?" to Riley. Instead, by the time Jack and Riley had moved to the bedroom, they'd covered everything from the weather to the honeymoon to the oil market. Conspicuous by its absence was an in-depth discussion about Hayley or her mom, other than the rehashing of what had been said before. They were in a curious kind of limbo until the next day, and discussing what-ifs and maybes would serve little purpose.

Riley got into bed first, lying back on the pillows and

staring up at the ceiling. His cell phone was in his hand, and he nervously turned it over and over.

Jack reached over and took the cell in a quick move before Riley could argue. He placed it on the table, climbed into bed, and stopped anything Riley was going to say in protest with a searching, breath-stealing kiss. The connection wasn't the kind of kiss that served as a prelude to sex; it was just comforting, easy, and right.

"There's nothing we can do tonight." Riley closed his eyes and rolled onto his side away from Jack, then scooted back so he could be the little spoon.

Six foot plus of muscled man needed his support, and Jack would be there whenever it was needed. Whether either of them would sleep was debatable, but at least they were together.

CHAPTER 4

Riley leaned against the cold wall of the shower, his back flat to the tiles and the water hot against his chest and legs. Being woken from a fitful sleep by the sun shining through open drapes was not a good start to any day. Added to which, Jack was missing from the bed, and it did nothing for his nerves about the morning ahead.

Exhaustion was clouding the edges of his thoughts, and even after two cups of hot black coffee, it was all he could do to stand upright in the walk-in shower. A note on Jack's pillow. The simple missive read "Taylor-Wood restless—back soon" and was enough to explain why Jack wasn't still asleep next to him.

Riley sent up a quick thought. He hoped the horse was going to be okay. More than halfway through her pregnancy, Taylor-Wood was restless and seemingly in need of Jack's touch. He knew exactly how she felt— minus the pregnant part. He wanted Jack's arms around him now, and he squashed the irrational jealousy he felt for a horse. Jack had this way of smoothing the jagged peaks and troughs of Riley's emotions, settling him with calm control.

Take the news Riley could have fathered a child, for instance. That little nugget of information would be enough to have some partners running for the hills, but all Jack had said was that everything would be all right.

Riley desperately wanted to believe him. But how could things be the same again? Was he a father? Had Lexie left college pregnant with his baby? Who was this great-aunt? Why hadn't Lexie told him? If the kid was alone in the world, did it even matter if Hayley was his or not?

Riley didn't remember exchanging an awful lot of information with Lexie about any family she might have had, but he did remember the weekend he'd taken her home to the Hayes mansion with absolute clarity. Lexie was his rage against the machine. His way of showing Gerald, the man he'd thought was his father, that he could make something of himself and find a nice, well-brought-up girl all on his own.

His mom had been civil, Gerald had been suspiciously quiet, Jeff hadn't even been at home, and Eden had been young and chatty. Riley was surprised Eden couldn't remember Lexie; hell, it wasn't as if he took girls home on a daily basis. Then again, Eden had been a teenager in her own world. Lexie hadn't been the daughter of family friends. She had been all Riley's and very different. She didn't talk Paris fashion or to-die-for shoes with Eden, and she certainly didn't fawn all over him for what he had or for what his family had.

He hadn't managed to sleep with her on date one. She had thrown his initial clumsy, drunken pass back in his face with an icy-cold look of disdain, and that had sealed her fate as his next conquest. Incredibly bright, funny and sassy, she was just exactly what a young guy who wanted for nothing needed.

She was a challenge.

Riley remembered dark brown hair, wide blue eyes, and a body to drool over encased in tight denim and a cut off T-shirt that ended just below her ample breasts. He also recalled her shutting him out of her room, naked, after she came back from classes to find him lounging on her bed.

It had taken a long time and many underhanded processes to get into Lexie's pants, but it had been so worth it. She was enthusiastic in bed, and everything Riley wanted in a partner at that time. Being bi meant he had the pick of everyone, but girls were where it was at when he was at college, his fumbling with boys no more than mutual masturbation when drunk.

Jack had been Riley's real first male, and his only now, for the rest of Riley's natural life. Jack was his, and he was Jack's.

Lexie had shown him what monogamy could potentially be like. Not that they were in love for real; it was the kind of affection and attraction that lust caused, and when she left, he was over her in a few days.

Now he looked back, Lexie reminded him of Jack. He didn't know where that thought had come from, but it lingered even as he began to wash his hair. She'd had the same independence of thought and an identical loyalty. Riley didn't think he could love any single person more than Jack Campbell-Hayes. But Lexie had captured his twenty-year-old soul, fed his mind, and made him think. She'd helped him question what impact Hayes Oil had on the world and had sown the first seeds of doubt in his head.

The relationship had only lasted three months. He had efficiently and tidily ended it after sleeping with two girls from his economics class in quick succession, probably one of his only regrets in life outside of his fucked-up family. Copious amounts of anonymous campus sex smoothed the edges after she left.

Lexie had sent him an email saying she had to transfer colleges. He had read between the lines. She hadn't wanted him. That much was clear, but it was cool because he'd replaced her quickly.

Good for her, he thought with no small amount of self-deprecation. Hell, what if she had overlooked the drinking and the sex with other girls and stayed at his side much longer? She would have seen twenty-year-old Riley was a self-destructive, spoiled rich kid with nothing to offer her long-term. Hell, it had taken another eight years and the explosion of Jack into his life for him to really start growing up and to actually do something with his dreams.

If she'd known she was pregnant, though? How could she have left him?

She wasn't the type to sleep around. She'd not been any kind of virgin when they got together, but she'd had morals.

Unlike me.

Why would she leave him with just one email explaining she was finishing her studies at a Maine college and "thanks for the memories"? She had to know Riley would have moved mountains for a baby and paid any amount of money to make sure their child was happy.

He groaned inwardly as it hit him that perhaps that was exactly it. The frequency with which he had once solved problems in his life by using his endless supply of cash was frightening. Riley being rich as Croesus, she probably thought he would pay her off. Or, *shit*, that he would take the baby or, worse, want her to have an abortion. During the three months they'd been together he hadn't exactly been advertising himself as sensible and trustworthy. How would she have known he could be trusted?

Hell. He wouldn't even have trusted himself.

"Riley, you staying in here all day?"

The voice was loud over the noise of the water. Jack's voice. In fact, it was suddenly Jack's body inside the shower, stealing Riley's water. He hadn't even sensed the door open, let alone felt the coolness of the air outside the shower, and suddenly Jack was there.

His husband was all practicality and washing off the dust and smell of the barns; he didn't seem inclined to start anything physical or, in fact, to talk. Which, to be fair, was a good thing as Riley had a head full of problems.

They exchanged a good-morning kiss, shared the soap and a hug, and once rinsed, Jack turned off the water.

After they dressed, they sat nursing coffees in the kitchen. Riley's the third of the morning, and he was feeling antsy and restless.

"Taylor has an infection," Jack began conversationally.

Riley grunted in reply. It really was the most he could manage without shouting out why the fuck Jack thought talking about freaking horses was more important than talking about impending fatherhood. Irritation built in him, underlined by anger and his own inability to vocalize how he was feeling.

"Are you going to shave?" he finally snapped as he looked at Jack devouring toast like it was going out of fashion.

Jack stopped with a slice halfway to his mouth, and he stared at Riley with an incredulous look. "I'm going to do that in a while," he said carefully.

Riley bristled. The pitch of Jack's voice was his "shit, Riley is losing it" tone.

"We need to make a good impression, not look like we're cowboys who don't care."

Riley could have swallowed his words even as he said them. Jack was the cowboy here, certainly not Riley. Riley still hadn't lost the city's edge, so by implication, he was belittling Jack.

To his credit, Jack didn't rise to the comment. He simply placed the toast carefully on the counter and inhaled.

Riley saw the rise of his chest and winced.

"Do you want to do this now?" Jack asked. "Is that what you need? You want a discussion on cowboys who care in the kitchen of my momma's house?"

Shit. Bringing Donna into this wasn't fair. Riley loved Donna, and he loved this house. His gut twisted, and he stood quickly, pulled himself to his full height, and crossed his arms over his chest. "Don't bring your momma into this."

Jack took a step forward so they were toe to toe, and looked up at him. "I'm not arguing with you, Riley."

"Then go and shave."

"I've been up since three. I. Am. Eating. Breakfast." Each one of Jack's words was punctuated with careful precision.

"Why couldn't Donna go to see Taylor?"

Shit, what was he doing? Why was he even going down this route? He could feel his inner child, petulant and whiny, and it wasn't attractive. What had happened to being a grown man?

"Momma spent the night with the vet," Jack spat the word *vet*, leaving no uncertainty as to what he thought of that. Unspoken was "the horses are mine to watch over."

This effectively closed off every single argument in Riley's head, and frustrated, he snapped, "Well, *I* needed you."

Jack moved quicker than Riley had seen before, and Riley was briefly off balance and then pinned hard against the nearest wall in an instant. Jack nudged his legs apart until Riley had slumped down enough to make them equal in height. Riley went from pissed to hard-as-freaking-steel in seconds.

God, what it did to him when Jack got all alpha male on his ass.

"I get you're freaking out, okay?"

Riley just blinked, and Jack gripped his hands harder.

"Okay?" he repeated.

"Okay."

"But what we don't need this morning is an argument over some not really important shit. Right?"

Jack's lips were just there. A single millimeter between them, and an upswell of emotion flooded Riley. He didn't want an argument. Jeez, he didn't even want *sex*. He just wanted to get this whole visit out of the way and know for sure what they were doing. The waiting was killing him.

He wanted a kiss. He moved enough to press his lips to Jack's, and to give him his due, Jack didn't back away. It was Riley's apology for losing it, and it was a plea for affection and support.

Jack knew him too well. The kiss deepened until an

amused laugh broke them apart. Jack pulled back and rested his forehead against Riley's. "You all right?" he asked gently, and Riley closed his eyes briefly, then opened them.

"I want it done," he replied.

"You and me both, Het-boy."

A chuckle made them separate, and they turned to face Eden, the source of the sound, who had her back to them, filling a mug with coffee.

"Hey, Eden." Riley didn't ask the obvious question about why the hell his little sister was here so early. He knew she was here for him, and for Jack, but most of all for Hayley.

She turned to look at them and blew on the hot drink, peering over the rim of the mug. "I didn't sleep one minute last night thinking on what's happening. Wish they'd hurry up already," she grouched, then narrowed her eyes at Jack. "You gonna shave, cowboy?"

CHAPTER 5

It was actually a little after nine when the plume of dust from a cab on the long drive leading to the D indicated the arrival of Riley's future.

He had thought to call his mom and Jim, but he put the cell down as quickly as he'd picked it up. Eden told them she and Donna had decided to keep the news confined to Riley and Jack, and for a while, that was what Riley wanted to do. He wasn't sure he could handle his mom and the arrival of a potential daughter all in the space of an hour.

Cup of coffee number five was long past, but Eden had shut him down by tipping the rest of the pot down the sink.

Jack had shaved and dressed in his best jeans and a startlingly white shirt. He looked gorgeous, sexy, and every inch the gentleman rancher. The cowboy inside had been tamed to within an inch.

Riley glanced down at what he was wearing—a charcoal Armani suit, a white shirt, and a dark blue-and-gold tie—remnants of his life in the tower at Hayes Oil. The suit had been in a garment bag pushed to the back of his closet. Too many memories were attached to the clothes to make them something he wanted to see every day. He'd become too used to dressy denim and fitted shirts to go back to the restrictions of a suit, shirt, and tie. Now, even for his consultation meetings, he attended in dress pants and a button-down.

"Do I look okay?" He needed someone, *anyone*, to tell

him.

"You look like a sensible businessman," Jack replied just as Eden and Donna chorused "Fine!"

"Which is it? Is it just fine? Is it too much? Should I change?"

"Riley. You look like a PTA daddy. Okay?"

Trust Jack to say the thing that made Riley choke up. A daddy? Him?

The cab drew up in the dusty courtyard and parked between Jack's truck and his own 4x4. Two people climbed out: one an older woman, clearly the great-aunt, who stood and looked at the house, plus a second, much smaller person.

Riley held his breath and reached blindly for Jack's hand, interlacing their fingers and gripping tight. Hand in hand they exited the house and stood at the bottom of the stairs.

The great-aunt took the few steps nearer. The child by her side was a small scrap of humanity with the biggest brown eyes Riley had ever seen, and she simply stared at him.

Riley had never felt so tall in his life before, and using Jack's hand to balance, he hunkered down to kneel so he would be at her height.

"Riley Hayes? My name is Sophie McGuire," the woman said, but Riley couldn't talk to her. He was so focused on the child, on Hayley, and he ignored her.

"Hi, Hayley," he said, releasing his hold on Jack's hand. "How you doing?" He added a smile.

She hid momentarily behind Sophie, who gently encouraged her to step forward.

Riley had his first good look at the beautiful child. She was the image of Eden at that age, with brown eyes and blonde locks that fell nearly to her waist, curly and shining in the bright sunlight. There was stubbornness to the lift of her chin, and while Riley could see that in his own features every time he looked in the mirror, she was also very much her momma's child.

"Are you my daddy?" she finally asked.

"Yes, he is," Sophie interrupted.

Her tone dared Riley to deny Hayley's parentage.

The question hovered between them, despite what Sophie said, but there was no hesitation in Riley as he answered. "Yes, sweetheart, I am."

Jack joined Riley by crouching low.

"So, I can stay?" Hayley asked warily, looking from her great-aunt Sophie, then to Riley and Jack.

"Of course you can, baby," Riley said. "This is Jack, my husband."

"Hi, Hayley," Jack responded.

"She was right, then?" Sophie snorted softly. "Could be worse, I s'pose."

She was close enough for Riley to hear, and he wondered why she was leaving her niece with them if she disapproved of him and Jack. Tension curled inside him.

"Two daddies," he said. "And this is your Aunty Eden and Jack's mom, Donna."

"Uh-huh," Hayley said carefully and looked between Eden and Donna.

"Hello, Hayley," Eden said quickly. "We met yesterday."

"I remember," Hayley replied. She was staring at

Donna and looked as if she was going to add something, but Sophie talked over her.

"Mr. Hayes," she began, "Lexie wanted me to look out for Hayley until I could pass her on to you."

"Campbell-Hayes," Jack commented quickly as he stood and stared pointedly at the woman.

She inclined her head at the words, long white hair falling about her face, and then passed Riley a folder she'd been gripping in her hand. "These are papers from the lawyers dealing with Lexie's estate. Hayley's details are inside the folder."

"Thank you," Riley said.

Everyone stood quietly for what seemed like hours but was only probably a few seconds, no one quite knowing what to say, the pause pregnant with questions. Finally, Donna managed to push the conversation along.

"I imagine Hayley would like to see inside her new house," she encouraged.

Riley snapped awake like he'd been in a daze. "Of course! You want to see inside, Hayley?" he said quickly.

Donna offered her a hand, and trustingly, Hayley took it before looking back briefly at Sophie with a small smile. Riley saw affection on his daughter's face, but Hayley made no move to hug Sophie.

"Bye, Aunt Sophie," she said, and allowed Donna to lead her up to the porch.

Jack placed himself between the front door and the aunt, and, at somewhat of an impasse, Riley didn't know what to say.

As soon as the door shut, Sophie's mask of icy indifference fell and true emotion showed on her face.

Riley saw sadness and concern. Her eyes wet with tears, she clasped her hands together.

"I didn't want to do this," she said quickly, "but Lexie said she would be safer with you than with her sister, and I'm not getting any younger."

This was possibly the oddest situation Riley had ever found himself in, and the most uncomfortable. "Safer?" he asked as he focused on that single word.

"When Lexie was ill, her sister, Sarah, took over a lot of Hayley's care. They are close—*were* close," she added, correcting herself immediately. "It was always intended for Hayley to be with her father after Lexie was told her cancer was too aggressive… too advanced." She closed her eyes briefly, and Riley could hear the grief in the words. There was a strange tightness in his chest at the thought that if Lexie had lived, he might never have known he was a daddy. "There wasn't time for her to…. There's a letter in there that explains it all."

"Thank you." It was all he could say.

He didn't ask why the sister didn't have custody; he didn't question why Lexie wanted him to have Hayley. In fact, he was incapable of thinking past getting into the house to see his daughter. He just thanked whoever was listening for bringing Hayley to his door.

"There are bags in the cab," Sophie said. "I wonder if someone could help me?" Jack stepped forward, then Riley, and in less than a minute, everything Riley knew of Hayley's entire life was sitting on the D's drive.

"Would you be so kind as to cover the cost of the cab?" Sophie asked.

Riley immediately pulled out his wallet and grabbed

every single bill he had. He didn't bother counting. There was probably more than she needed. He would pay her everything for the single fact that she had cared enough to bring his daughter to him.

"How are you getting home?" he asked, concerned.

"The cab is waiting," she said.

"I could organize a car."

"I have my arrangements made," she said simply. Squaring her shoulders, she looked Riley straight in the eyes. "Promise me that you will look after her."

"I will. I do."

"Lexie's sister…. It isn't right for her to have Hayley, and Lexie knew that. Lexie always told me you were the one who should take the child."

"I'm her dad," Riley said unnecessarily.

"Lexie wasn't sure."

"Sure of what? Sure Riley was the dad?" Jack sounded confused.

"She wasn't sure it mattered if Riley was the dad or not. She didn't imagine Riley would want her—"

"What the hell?" Riley couldn't hold back the instant and visceral reaction.

He might have been an idiot at twenty, but everyone grew up, so who the hell was Lexie to think something so plainly awful?

"Until…." Sophie waved a hand between Riley and Jack.

"Until?"

"It isn't my place to say, Mr. Hayes—"

"Campbell-Hayes," Riley interrupted, and Sophie inclined her head to acknowledge the mistake.

"She said you were settled in whatever you are settled in." She looked uncomfortable momentarily. "I don't know what's worse—Lexie's sister and her problems or you and your... unconventional... relationship."

Riley narrowed his eyes and wondered how far Jack was going to let this go before he lost his temper.

"Still," Sophie carried on, oblivious to what reaction she was engendering, "it remains the lesser of two evils."

* * * * *

As the cab disappeared up the long drive, avoiding the potholes and cracks in the dry ground, Jack turned to Riley with a grim look on his face.

"What the fuck was *that* all about?"

All Riley could do was shrug. He really had no idea at all.

The two men went into the house. Hayley was chatting about hair and playing with her own by twisting it around her tiny hands.

Riley stopped dead. They looked so alike, his sister and his beautiful daughter. And they seemed to be connecting. Irrational jealousy spiked in him, and he shook himself free of it.

"How about your daddy shows you your room?" Eden said gently.

Hayley looked at him expectantly, and he dropped the folder onto the kitchen table before taking her extended hand.

Donna and Eden were talking, but once the door shut between the kitchen and the hall, it was just Riley and

Hayley. He paused in the hallway. A bedroom... he hadn't spent any time thinking about that. But his responsibility, the change in his life, his daughter losing her momma—those were the things he had focused on, not on providing a little girl a haven in among the rough-and-tough of the D.

The D was a working ranch. He and Jack shared Jack's two rooms; Donna's was upstairs, although she appeared to spend most nights from dusk until dawn at Neil's house. Still, it was her room, and that only left Beth's or Josh's old rooms at the back of the house.

Out of Jack's two siblings, Riley guessed Beth's room was likely more girly than Josh's, and the window faced the back paddocks. Decision made, he took a right and went down the short corridor to the end, to the door marked with a carved name.

"This was Beth's old room. She's Jack's sister," He crouched down again. "I've not seen inside it, and I don't know if it's pink or girly or anything. But whatever it's like, we can fix it up, okay? You can have any kind of bedroom you want."

Hayley nodded, and then, standing tall, Riley pushed his way in.

Well, it wasn't pink. In fact it wasn't really much of anything. A simple room with wooden floors and a large double bed with a carved headboard. A chest of drawers with a small mirror and a desk in the corner completed the look. Clearly, Donna had this room set up as some kind of guest room, judging by the simple furnishings.

"It's big," Hayley said, her eyes wide as she circled to see the whole room. "Bigger than my momma's and mine together."

"We can change anything you want," Riley offered quickly, and then he watched bemused as Hayley clambered onto the bed and lay back to stare at the ceiling.

"It's kind of cool," she offered in the simple manner of a child. Riley sat on the edge of the bed; the weight of him caused Hayley to roll slightly. She giggled and leaned on one arm to look at him. "You're really heavy," she said with a laugh.

"Guess I am," he agreed.

"Way tall. Momma said my daddy was really tall."

Riley could have sat there and cried. Lexie had spoken about him? Lexie had known he was Hayley's biological dad but had never thought to contact him? Why had she done that? Instead, he pushed past the hurt and confusion and smiled.

"You may get way tall as well," he said.

"I don't wanna be *that* tall." Her eyes widened again and a look of horror settled on her face. Riley laughed.

"I get to see over everyone."

"So not a good thing."

"I can reach Donna's cookie shelf," he confided with a smile and a wink. Hayley's eyes widened, and he thought maybe he had scored a point in his favor.

"I could get a chair," she said thoughtfully. "If the cookies were good enough."

Riley was alternating between pride and horror. Hayley, *his daughter*, was so direct. She was talking to him almost like she was in an adventure. He wondered how much of it was bravado and how much damage had been done by her mom dying.

"I'm sorry. You know…" he began, and then he didn't really know where he was going. What level should he pitch this at? She was eight, but she seemed so grown-up. Best he was direct, he thought. "Sorry about your mom," he finally said as simply as he could.

Hayley pulled her lower lip with her teeth, and Riley saw a couple of gaps. He wondered quickly if she was going to cry and then wondered how the hell he was going to manage to handle the tears of a little girl.

"She was ill for a long time, but she was mostly happy."

That seemed a contradiction in terms to Riley, but it must have made sense to Hayley. "I'm so sorry. Your mom was a very good person." He vocalized the thoughts but didn't mention the overwhelming anger that Lexie hadn't called him. "Mostly I'm sorry I didn't know about you."

"Why do you think mom didn't tell you about me?"

Jeez, a leading question if there ever was one.

What should he say? He didn't have a freaking clue why Lexie had chosen to have Hayley on her own. Was he angry? Or was he sad? Maybe he should explain he had been more than 80 percent selfish idiot when he was twenty, and he was surprised the relationship with Lexie had lasted even three months.

Suddenly it was very important to him—vital, even—that he told Hayley her mom must have had reasons. He had to push his own anger and disappointment to one side where his baby girl was concerned. Nothing would tarnish the memory of her momma, and he was ready to accept every ounce of responsibility. Lexie must have had her reasons to keep Hayley away from him.

"Your mom and I were both so young, and I wasn't the best person to know then. Not exactly the best boyfriend ever."

"'Cause you wanted to marry a man?" she asked directly.

"I wasn't…. I hadn't…."

"Mom always said I ask difficult questions," Hayley interrupted with a grin.

A grin big enough to worm its way into Riley's heart. His daughter was intelligent, apparently, and God, did he love that. He laughed. "Are you sure you're only eight?"

"Nearly nine."

So serious.

"When is your birthday?" Jeez, he didn't even know that. Grief gripped him. He had missed so much—but he ruthlessly pushed those negative feelings down.

"September 6," she said, "so I'm nearly nine."

This talking-to-his-daughter business was easy. She was a precocious eight- nearly nine-year-old who made him smile.

In a tone Riley remembered Eden using when she was little, Hayley said, "I saw horses out there yesterday, and Momma said you would get me a pony for my birthday. So can I have one?"

CHAPTER 6

When Riley and Hayley made it back out to the kitchen, there was a pile of paperwork on the table and a jumble of cases at the door. Jack was thumbing through the papers, reading; Donna was making new coffee; and Eden was pacing. All movement stopped when Riley pushed open the kitchen door. Everyone looked at him expectantly.

"I put Hayley in Beth's old room, but it isn't very...." He circled his finger to indicate everything he didn't know about little girls and what they wanted in their bedrooms.

"Okay," Eden responded quickly and looked at Hayley. "Well, we can go girly shopping. Would you like that?"

Hayley nodded, but Riley saw a hint of sadness in her that just broke his heart.

"You can have anything you want," he offered quickly. Then, seeing Eden's look of warning, added, "Within reason, of course. Um, to make it your own room."

"Dad said I can have a pony," she announced quickly, and Riley cringed as he caught Jack's questioning expression.

"It's her birthday in a few weeks," Riley said in his defense.

Jack grinned and shook his head. "We can get a pony. Do you ride, Hayley?"

"I tried once at a fair."

"So riding lessons as well," Eden said seriously.

"I can do that," Jack offered.

Riley smiled with relief. He could ride, but Jack could

ride.

"Shall we get your stuff put away, sweetie?" Donna asked.

"Do you want me to help?" Riley asked immediately, even though what he really wanted was to take a breath and think.

"Nah, we'll do it." Eden laughed, hooking her hand with Hayley and winking conspiratorially. "Girls' stuff. Though, if you two guys could bring in the bags...."

* * * * *

As soon as the bags were in Hayley's room, Riley slumped in his chair in the kitchen and buried his head in his hands on the table.

I can't do this.

"You can do this," Jack said. Riley cursed his husband for knowing exactly what was going through his head. "There are just a few things you need to do. The lawyers say they need a DNA test on record."

Irritation bloomed inside Riley. "She's mine, Jack. Even a complete stranger can see that."

"It's an official thing. Stops anyone from trying to put a claim on her."

"Lexie's sister, Sarah, you mean."

Jack sighed and shuffled through the papers in front of him, pulling out the relevant page. "This is kind of sad reading about Lexie. No parents, just a sister, Sarah. Sarah's married but has no kids. Couple of cousins and this great-aunt, Sophie McGuire from Abilene. But as far as I can make out, it was Lexie and Hayley mostly on their own."

"Shit, Jack." Riley couldn't believe Lexie had chosen to isolate them away from him. Had she really hated him that much? Grief welled inside him at how much he had missed with Hayley. He was determined to fix it all. She had him and Jack and Eden, and God, all of Jack's extended family, and Sandra and Jim.

Jack continued. "Hayley has some money in an account—her mom's account balances put into one. There's just over $7,000, with some kind of deduction for lawyer fees and a burial."

"Those lawyers used Hayley's inheritance to bury her own momma?" Riley sat up, horrified.

Jack nodded. "We can replace it for her," he said gently.

"Fucking leeches."

"I called Josh," Jack started.

Riley could have smacked himself. He'd forgotten Josh was a lawyer and therefore tacitly included in the *leech* analogy. "I didn't mean Josh was a leech," he said quickly.

"I know you didn't." Jack brushed the words away with a quirk of his lips. "Anyway, he's coming over a bit later to check out all the papers and give us some advice."

"That's good." Riley pulled the pile of documents toward him and looked down at the jumble of legal words that swam on the paper.

Jack cleared his throat in that "I've got something to tell you" way Riley had grown to hate.

"What else?" he asked. He didn't really want to know because Jack couldn't look him in the eyes. This was clearly something serious.

"There's not much else here. Except the birth certificate and, um…."

"Um?"

"School transfer papers."

"Shit," Riley sat upright. "School! We need to get her to a school. Or do we have to get a private tutor? God, Jack, what am I—what do normal parents do?"

Silence. Jack passed the school reports over. Riley glanced at them, and certain words jumped right out at him. His kid—Hayley—well, she was bright.

"Okay, schools. She's eight. We can ask around about schools, and we can afford the best." He began pacing the small kitchen from scarred counter to oven and back again.

"We can worry about schooling later." Jack held out a hand to stop the pacing. "Let's just get Hayley settled in."

"Riley?"

Eden's voice broke into Riley's thoughts, and he looked up to see Hayley standing at Eden's side and holding an envelope out to him.

Eden's expression held a sadness he hadn't seen in a while, and Riley was instantly worried. What was wrong? Was there something wrong with Hayley?

Jeez, I can't do this. I'm not a dad.

He was a grown man who had no experience with kids other than his brother's, and the nanny looked after them.

A nanny? Maybe I need to get a nanny?

"Riley?" Eden's voice interrupted his musings and he snapped back to the here and now. "Hayley says this letter is for you from a box of her mom's stuff," Eden explained.

Riley took the plain white envelope from his daughter carefully, like she was offering him a grenade. He pulled it to his chest and sat back down in his chair.

"Mom said to tell you that you should read the letter," Hayley said as if from memory. She subtly moved to stand at Riley's side, her small hand touching his arm. Riley turned in his chair to face her. "She wrote letters to me too. Lots of them. She said it would make me understand."

"Oh, Hayley." Eden had a hand to her lips, blinking furiously as her eyes filled with tears.

"Mom said to give it to you when I found you. And I did. I found you," Hayley said simply.

She left Riley's side then and pulled at Eden's hand, and together, the two girls moved into the hallway. Suddenly, Jack and Riley were very alone.

"You read it," Riley said instantly and slid the letter across the table.

Jack pushed it back. "It's yours, Riley."

"I can't."

"Take it outside and read it on your own." Riley started to interrupt, but Jack just kept talking. "I'll be here for when you want to talk, and I can go and help the girls. Okay?"

Riley was confused by Jack's words and his reaction. Part of him wanted Jack to fix this for him like he fixed the rest of Riley's complicated life. The other part wondered why the hell this was happening to him, to Riley Hayes. *Campbell-Hayes.* Since when was he unable to at least face the shit his family landed him in?

"I'll be in the barn," he said tiredly, and only stopped his exit when Jack laid a hand on his arm.

"I'm here," his husband said, and for a second Riley leaned in to Jack and bumped shoulders.

It was enough touch to reassure him, and Riley felt braver for it.

* * * * *

Their barn.

The place where Riley and Jack had talked, come to terms with each other, and had some of the hottest sex Riley had ever known. Every beam, every wall held memories, and there was even a stash of supplies hidden in a wooden box in the corner. It was *their* place away from the house, and the empty barn felt safe and secure. Though it still smelled of hay and horses, it had an aura of disuse. He settled himself in the corner near the box, his back against the wall and his long legs stretched out in front of him.

The letter sat on his lap, and for a while he just stared at it. He tried to consider worst-case scenarios, but the only one he could come up with was that somehow, in this letter, it was revealed Hayley wasn't his. He closed his eyes and sent a prayer up to whoever looked down on him that, just for once, he could be strong enough to take whatever he was told and not feel overwhelming guilt for his family's actions.

Maybe there was an innocent reason. Lexie could have left without even knowing she was pregnant, and it might have nothing to do with him or his family.

Taking a deep breath, he slid a finger under the side of the seal and opened the envelope. Two pieces of notepaper fell into his hand, along with a bundle of photos tied with a ribbon, and a tiny key and heart on a chain. He remembered the chain—something he had bought for Lexie as a Valentine's gift. She had loved it and worn it every day. He clenched a fist around it, and, summoning every bit of strength and courage he had, he opened the letter.

Handwritten in black ink, with sloping, regular lines and looped *g*'s, it was a simple and beautiful thing to look at. After smoothing out the letter on his lap, Riley began to read. It wasn't a polished letter. The sentences were short, as if thoughts had just spilled onto the paper, but on the second page, emotion showed in a line not perfectly straight and sentences holding more feelings than actual thoughts.

Dear Riley,

There is so much I want to say here, but I know nothing I write will let you totally forgive me for what I did. So I go into this with a heavy heart.

I should call you. Or visit. But I can't. This illness was aggressive, and it came on me so fast. So the time for talk passed. I've gone from someone with plenty of tomorrows to being too sick to think rationally.

There's one thing I need to write, though, and it's vital I get it out of the way first. In a way, it's the most important of everything. I have a sister, Hayley's Aunty Sarah, and I'm sure you're questioning why I didn't have her take custody of Hayley. It's important you make sure she never gets custody in any way over Hayley. It isn't Sarah I worry about, but her husband, who makes everyone's life hell. He's bad news. And if you do nothing else, then please promise me you will protect Hayley with your life.

God, how melodramatic does that sound? My will states Hayley should be with her daddy, but I know things can go wrong.

I get this is a big thing to ask, but I think, when you get to know Hayley, you'll see how easy it is to love her.

Riley blinked at the words. He didn't need to get to know Hayley. In the space of half an hour, she had become part of who he was.

I've had to go. I didn't want to. I don't want to. The doctors don't give out time left anymore, but when I secretly read "three months" on my notes... well, let's just say they seem to know what they're saying. It wasn't enough time to reconnect with you or to smooth the way as the treatments are kind of rough. I talked a lot to Hayley about you, though, so she knows.

Just to make it clear, Hayley is your daughter. There's no doubt about that, and I hope you believe me without needing tests or fighting it. She needs to know her daddy now, and you and your husband seem settled and happy. It will be good for her. And for you, I hope.

No. He didn't need tests. She was his.

Hayley is a very special little girl. She's not quite you and not quite me, but a mix of us both. In fact, thinking back on your little sister, I think Hayley looks a lot like her. There are some photos with this letter for each of the years she was mine alone, and you will see what I mean.

I don't know you now or what kind of man you have really become. You won't believe this, but I loved you when we made Hayley, and that's the important thing, I think. I read an article about a man starting ethical exploration, and he is my *Riley, the one I saw when you thought I couldn't see inside you.*

I told Hayley you live on a ranch with your husband, and she focused immediately on horses. She has always wanted a pony, but a secretary's wage doesn't stretch that far. I know what you're like with your money, but don't spoil her. For a quiet life, though, I think you should get her one. She is a very determined child, and I read that animals are good for helping with emotional problems. My guess is she's already asked you, and I know for a fact you won't be able to say no. She has this way of asking that breaks your heart sometimes.

I always talked about how I met you from the very moment she could understand. The lectures, the café, the gorgeous boy who swept me off my feet, even how tall you are and the color of your eyes. I've written letters to Hayley over the last few months, and I want her to get them as she grows up. I got the idea from a book I read, and I liked the thought of her getting a letter before her prom, or for the first day of college. I deposited them at the bank, and all the details will be with the lawyer.

I told her everything but your name, but I was going to as soon as she asked when she was older. You were never a secret.

Keeping Hayley away from you wasn't a decision I

made lightly. A father should know his children, and every day I wanted to tell you. I have no excuses other than I didn't ever want to lose her. I thought if you knew about her, then I might lose her. It was selfish, but I hope you can forgive me.

I know you're saying to yourself that we could have been a family, but it would never have worked. There would never be a place for me in your life. I was never going to be the person at your side. I could have tried to fit in, but I would have ended up hating my life and you.

I didn't know I was pregnant until after I left. I promise you I didn't. Do you believe me?

I want what is best for Hayley, and I know that is you.

I tried hard to give her good memories. It's your turn now.

Please.

Lexie xx

Did he believe she didn't know she was pregnant with his baby when she left? Did he believe Hayley was his daughter?

Of course he did. He believed Lexie. So yes. *God, yes.* He would take his turn.

He reread the letter, weighing accusation against truth and the past Riley against the person he was now. Indignation at the thought he couldn't have made a good dad at twenty was momentary. He didn't even have clear memories of his college years; most were edged with alcohol. Then after college, embroiled in the vitriol and hate that surrounded the family in the old Hayes mausoleum, what place would there have been for a child?

In a daze he clambered to stand, weaving in place at the head rush. He hated the pain in his heart that he hadn't been good enough for his child. Lexie was right. She'd always had the uncanny ability to see right through him, and his family would have destroyed her and a child. That was who they'd been.

So Riley needed to do what Lexie asked. Buy Hayley a pony, but refrain from spoiling her further with money, and most of all, love her like his own.

That last part, he thought, would be very easy.

CHAPTER 7

"Riley? Come to bed."

Jack's voice echoed in the hallway.

"I can't. What if she wakes up and can't remember where she is? She could get upset."

"Her door is open. We'll hear." Jack gestured to the open bedroom door where Riley hovered.

"But our door is always shut," Riley was quick to point out.

"So we'll leave it open," Jack offered with a shrug.

"You'd do that?"

"It's a door."

"But…." *What about kissing and cuddling and the danger of someone walking in on us?*

"But nothing. You're a dad now, Riley. Dads leave the door open for their kids in case they're needed. Are you coming to bed?"

"In ten or so."

Jack embraced him from behind, and Riley leaned back into the hold, turning his head to share a quick kiss.

When Jack left, Riley couldn't move. He leaned against the doorjamb of his new daughter's room and stared in at the small shape under the covers. The drapes were pulled shut, and the only light into the room came from the dim bulb in the hall. Hayley hadn't even asked for a nightlight. Luke and Annabelle still slept with nightlights, maybe due to a psychological problem after losing their dad. Jeff might have been Riley's brother, but he was one hell of a shitty father.

Jesus. Who's to say I'll be any better?

He shared the same genes as Jeff—well, half of them anyway. Riley had too much of his natural father in him to be entirely like Jeff.

That thought sent a snap of memory into his head. "Shit." *Jim and Mom.*

He stood upright and then waited to see if his muttered expletive woke Hayley. She didn't move, and in the blink of an eye, he was moving to his and Jack's room.

Jack was in bed, leaning back against the carved headboard, with a copy of *Quarter Horse News* in his hand. He looked up with a smile when Riley entered the room. "She sleeping okay?" he asked.

Riley nodded, and then, because he didn't know how else to word it, he simply said, "Mom and Jim. I need to tell them their son is a daddy. How the fuck am I going to do that?"

Jack simply passed him the phone. "Call them and invite them for breakfast," he said patiently. Riley held the handset tight and worried his lower lip with his teeth. "Riley?"

Of course Jack would wonder why he was hesitating. "How do I tell them? What will they think?"

"You're their son. And it will be an easy journey to acceptance for them."

Riley listened to Jack's words, contemplating the fact his husband had such a lyrical way with words. Sometimes, Jack opened his mouth and the lazy drawl of a cowboy came out; other times he said the most amazingly insightful things that just tied up all the indecision that plagued Riley and threw it in the trash. Riley often thought he was married to two different men—and he loved both sides of Jack.

Jack wasn't reacting anywhere near the way Riley imagined he would. At dinner, Jack had already been planning which ranch to go to for the pony, and he'd agreed to put up shelves for the two bags of books Hayley had arrived with.

If Jack could accept everything so easily, then what was stopping Riley from feeling like he could do this? And why the hell was he hesitating about how to tell Jim and his mom, exactly? He should be able to handle that.

"Jim's going to kill me," he muttered.

Riley had found out Jim Bailey was his real father when he needed a blood transfusion. Jim had always known he was Riley's father. They had made inroads into reconciling those two facts, but Riley still didn't call him Dad. Dad was still Gerald, a man Riley had hated. He couldn't associate the word Dad with Jim and the easy relationship they had. *Dad* was a meaningless word to Riley, and he wished he could get away from feeling like he was going to be no better at fathering than Gerald had been.

"He's not going to kill you."

"Mom too."

Riley's relationship with his mom was stronger with every passing day, and he'd laid a lot of how he felt about her at Jim's feet. Sandra had changed so much. Still Texas aristocracy, but she was softening at the edges daily. Jim made his mom happy, and she deserved that. Added to that, Jim was now officially courting her, which kind of put Riley's world off balance.

Okay, so he still wasn't calling Jim "Dad," but there'd been too much water under the bridge for Riley and Jim, and too much time had passed. Would it be the same for Hayley and him?

"I don't know what to say to them." Riley couldn't think of where to start to explain to Jack.

"How about 'Mom, Jim, I'm a dad, and I want you to meet my beautiful daughter, Hayley.'"

Jack obviously thought he was being helpful or that Riley needed the mood lightened. Riley still had to make Jack see what was in his head.

He began carefully. "Do you know, when Jim was the Hayes Oil attorney, he had to deal with five separate paternity claims against me from three different women in the space of two years. Women I had never even met, let alone slept with." Riley sat down heavily on the bed next to Jack.

"Money breeds that kind of thing," Jack said in an offhand way.

Riley bristled at the accusation he heard in Jack's voice, and he rounded on his husband in an instant. "*What?*" he snapped. "Me fucking around?"

"No, jeez, Riley, calm down. I meant people will do anything for money."

Jack placed a hand on the base of Riley's spine and began a small circular motion, patiently letting Riley know he was there and supporting him.

Riley sighed and leaned back slightly into the touch. "None of them were true. To contact Jim now and admit I actually *am* a father…"

"I don't see what you—Wait, are you worried he'll be

disappointed?"

"Yes." That was exactly what he was thinking would happen. Dad or not, Jim's respect meant an awful lot to Riley.

"Just tell him the truth: Lexie was the one that got away, and you didn't know anything about Hayley."

Jack made it sound so easy.

"Easier said than done," Riley muttered.

Jack kept up with the gentle press of fingers on his back.

Sighing, Riley connected to Sandra's number, and she answered the call on the third ring.

"Hello?"

"Hi, Mom."

"Riley. Hello, darling. Is everything okay? It's late—"

"Would you and Jim come to breakfast tomorrow? There's something I'd like to talk to you both about."

Well, it wasn't exactly "I'm a dad," but at least he had a time and a place set in his head for the big reveal. He was hiding behind Hayley. Jim and his mom couldn't be sorry for what happened or think less of Riley once they met the gorgeous child, their granddaughter. Could they?

"Of course we can. What's wrong? Is it Eden?" Sandra sounded worried, and he heard the rumble of Jim's voice in the background.

"Riley?" Jim had clearly taken the phone from her, and his tone held an urgent question. "What's wrong?"

"Nothing's wrong. I'm just inviting my parents to breakfast."

"At midnight?" Jim sounded skeptical.

Riley wasn't winning this one at all. "Just try to get

here by nine. I have something I need to tell you."

There was a brief pause at the other end of the line, then Jim said, "Okay, son, we'll be there."

"Nine?"

"Nine."

Riley ended the call and breathed a sigh of relief. At least he had a reprieve of nine hours and the chance for sleep. He climbed into bed, then pulled the magazine from Jack's hands. He didn't lean in to kiss or initiate anything; he just needed sleep and to know Jack was there.

Jack seemed to get the message and leaned over to turn out the light. Riley sighed and pulled Jack close for a hug, but sleep eluded him even as Jack's breathing changed to the rhythm of slumber.

Riley tried relaxing each muscle in turn, inhaling his husband's scent and the cool nighttime Texas air, but it was a long time until sleep finally chased him down.

* * * * *

Sleep didn't last long.

"Riley."

"'M 'sleep," Riley mumbled.

"Riley." This time, Jack's voice was more insistent and pushed along by the tempting scent of coffee.

Riley managed to force open his eyes. "Whatimeisit?"

"Just after six. I brought coffee."

Riley groaned. He'd probably only been asleep a few minutes. Or at least it seemed like it.

Jack went on. "I'm out with Taylor. She's restless again."

"Horses. Okay."

"Are you getting up?"

"Jeez," Riley muttered and forced himself to scramble upright in the bed. "I'm up already."

Jack chuckled and then placed a gentle kiss to Riley's forehead. "Love you, Het-boy," he said softly as he left the room.

Showered and dressed, Riley was in the kitchen by six thirty, brewing more coffee and standing at the window of the silent house. He wondered what time Hayley would wake. He wondered if he should go and get her up. Wasn't that what dads did for their kids? It was too early now, but should he go in at seven or seven thirty and take her a drink? Not coffee, and water was too boring…. Inspired, he rooted in the cupboard and located the tin of hot chocolate he remembered was Donna's favorite. Hot chocolate would be good; kids liked chocolate. Maybe one of Donna's cookies as well? With a cookie and powder in a mug sitting on the table, he was done, so he sat down.

Then he stood up. Might as well get the breakfast stuff out as well.

That was how Jack found him. He came in through the main door, stamping dirt from his boots and bringing with him the scent of the outside. He eyed the array of food and raised an eyebrow. "How many are we feeding?"

* * * * *

Hayley woke a little after eight. With Eden back at her own apartment in the city and Donna with her vet at his place, Riley was left with a small child and absolutely no idea of what to do or say. Of course he was fully aware she needed to wash up, get dressed, brush her teeth, and then come to eat breakfast. He wasn't stupid. He just didn't know how to tell her. In the end, they stood eyeballing each other uncertainly for a good ten seconds before Hayley took control.

"Morning," she said brightly.

Hoisting her oversize PJs up, she clambered onto a tall stool next to where Riley was getting things ready to cook.

"Morning, Hayley," Riley answered quickly.

She leaned in and hugged him, and he responded quickly with his own hug. Then she sat back and pulled her knees up, perching precariously.

"Can we have pancakes?" she asked.

Riley smiled. A girl after his own heart. "We can. And we even have real maple syrup."

She wrinkled her nose. "Eww, that's too sweet. I like lemon. Do you have any lemon?"

"Lemon?" Riley tried to remember if Lexie had liked lemon on her pancakes. Who the hell had lemon on pancakes? There had to be some kind of rational explanation that a child of his wouldn't like syrup. "Lemon," he repeated faintly, completely aware he was coming over like some kind of defective parrot.

"We have lemon."

Donna's voice came from behind him, and he had never been so pleased to hear it. He spun to face her, then placed a hand near Hayley as her stool wobbled.

"Why don't you wash up and get dressed, Hayley, and let your dad take you to see the horses," Donna said quickly.

Riley kissed Donna on the cheek affectionately and waited as Hayley finished her cookie, climbed down, and disappeared out of the kitchen.

"Are you feeding that child cookies for breakfast?" Donna teased.

Riley squirmed. "Just to tide her over," he said quickly.

Donna chuckled and peered out of the window to the yard beyond. "Is Jack out with Taylor again?"

"She was restless, apparently."

"She's in her sixth month. It's always a strange time for them. Riley…."

"Yeah?"

"I know the timing is bad, but I wanted to ask you—no, *tell* you something."

That sounded ominous with a capital *O*. Why did Donna want to tell him something when Jack wasn't in the room? "Go on."

"There's no easy way to say this, but Neil asked me to move in with him, into the house attached to the clinic."

Riley could feel his eyes widen. Hell. Jack had only tolerated Neil Kendrick stepping out with his momma because he thought it wouldn't last long. And now they were moving in together? Why was Donna telling him? She should be talking directly to Jack.

She undoubtedly saw the reaction on his face and shook her head. "I want to ask you a favor, and you can say no if you like."

Riley's heart sank. He loved Donna. A slim, irrepressible force of nature, his mother-in-law had been so supportive about his problems and his relationship with her son, and now with Hayley. He already had some idea what she might ask him, and knowing Jack's temper, it was going to result in traveling down a very rocky road.

"What favor?" he asked, even though he thought he probably knew.

"Will you talk to Jack for me? I spoke to Josh yesterday and Beth over the weekend, but every time I try to talk to Jack, he closes down."

Riley listened to the words, but his head was filled with Hayley and his own life. So what he said next came out with no preparation and possibly verged on rude. "He's your son, Donna, and he's worried about you."

"Neil is a good man."

"Neil's only a bit older than Jack."

"He loves me, Riley. I love him."

She looked pale, and he hated what he was saying. God, he was repeating what Jack had said. He wasn't thinking about how *he* felt in all of this. He liked Neil. Yes, the veterinarian was young, but he was settled and educated, and he clearly adored Donna. Seemed like the guy was moving out of his small apartment and into the solidly built house attached to the clinic—a good thing, right? And it certainly indicated permanence. The age gap was a little much for Riley to get his head around, but who was he to judge? Who was Jack to judge? Two men being married wasn't exactly the normal way of going about things in the middle of Texas.

"There's no rush," Donna pointed out. "I spend every night with him, but to actually make it permanent... I'm not going to say it doesn't scare me after all this time on my own. Still, Jack's opinion—all of my children's opinions—mean so much to me."

Riley understood where she was coming from. What Hayley thought of him now and in some nebulous future—whether ex-playboy, blackmailer, and all-around people user—was something that had played on his mind last night as he lay in bed.

"I'll talk to him," Riley finally answered.

Donna smiled. She had a beautiful smile, and she certainly didn't look like a woman in her mid-fifties. She looked happy and rested and stunning.

"I'm ready," Hayley interrupted, and this one, Riley was happy about.

"Come on." He offered her a hand. "Let's go scare Jack."

* * * * *

"Your daughter?"

Simple words, not spoken with anything other than an expected amount of shock. As far as Sandra had been concerned, she never thought she'd get grandchildren from him, and it seemed Jim was on the same wavelength.

"Hi," Hayley said softly, and Riley watched carefully as Jim, *his dad*, sank to a crouch in front of her.

"Hello, Hayley."

Jim had been introduced as her granddad, Sandra as her grandmother, and Hayley stood there and took it all in with a happy expression in her beautiful brown eyes. Jim held out his arms and pulled her in for a close hug, and she went willingly.

As far as Riley had been able to make out, Lexie's parents were no longer alive. That meant Jim and Sandra would be her first real contact with grandparents, at least in a while. Riley observed the expressions flitting across his mom's face. Shock, disbelief, and then an aching tenderness. She bent over from her waist—Sandra was not one to go to her knees—and extended the hug between Jim and Hayley to include her too.

Breakfast was lively, a perfect start to the day. In deference to Hayley, Riley sat separate from Jack, but he missed his husband's solid presence at his side. The adults listened to her lively chatter for the hour they ate, chatted, and drank hot chocolate and coffee.

"Can I have a word, son?" Jim finally asked.

Riley looked quickly at Hayley, who was engrossed in talking about *Glee* with his mom and Donna. Jack caught his expression and inclined his head. Riley nodded back. Jack would keep an eye out for Hayley.

This was clearly going to be the lecture Jim didn't feel he could issue in front of Hayley. Following Jim out of the house and to the fence, Riley started to worry, but it seemed Jim was fixated on the technical aspects of the newest arrival to the ranch.

"I'm assuming you have someone looking at Hayley's paperwork?"

"She's mine," Riley answered instantly. What did Jim mean *paperwork*?

"I know, son, I don't doubt it for a single minute," Jim immediately responded. "What I mean is have you had a family lawyer dot the i's and cross the t's?"

"You're our family's lawyer, so I assumed you would do it."

"Someone else. Other than me. As the grandfather, it

wouldn't be right."

"Not yet. Josh said he'd look it over—"

"Jack's brother is a criminal lawyer. Promise me you'll get an expert out here."

"Okay. I will. Thanks."

"That isn't what I wanted to talk to you about, though."

Riley frowned. "It wasn't?"

Surely Hayley's arrival was the most important thing for everyone to concentrate on? Why was Jim going to broach another subject? In his near future, Riley already had an awkward discussion with his volatile husband about Donna and her younger lover. Why did people think he was capable of multitasking? Jeez, was Jim going to start talking about love and his sex life with Riley's mom? He didn't think he could handle that without the support of alcohol.

"Riley—" Jim paused. "—something has come to light at Hayes Oil, from 2007."

Dread flooded Riley at those words spoken in such a heavy, ominous tone. But it was nothing compared to what Jim said next.

"It's missing paperwork, signed documents, proof of blackmail. It's about Jeff. Jeff and you."

CHAPTER 8

Jack sat patiently in the kitchen, perched on a stool, able to watch his husband with Jim.

Riley's body language went from relaxed, to tense, to pissed, and on to resigned in the space of ten minutes. Jack had intimate knowledge of every single one of those reactions, and he wondered what the hell Jim was throwing at Riley.

"So I'm thinking we should have a barbecue or something," Donna said.

"A celebration," Sandra said. "Would you like that, Hayley? You could meet your cousins, Luke and Annabelle." Sandra was animated with her excitement, but all Jack could do was groan as she began to plan. Annabelle, fifteen and levelheaded, was fine, but her brother Luke? He was a twelve-year-old chip off Jeff's block. He'd thrown freaking big stones at Solo-Cal in her stall, causing the horse to become distressed with no way to escape. The last thing Jack wanted was that hell spawn anywhere near his horses. Then, as soon as he'd thought it, he immediately felt guilty. Of course, Luke's dad had died, his granddad as well, and his mom was working through chronic alcohol dependency. All of that probably played hell with his preteen hormones. Still, there was no excuse for what Jack had caught him doing to the horses last time they were here.

"Jack? What do you think? Should we have everyone over on Saturday? Get Josh and his kids, and Beth and her family, and Eden?"

"Whatever, Momma. It's your house," Jack offered distractedly.

The kitchen was suddenly silent, and Jack blinked back to the here and now. What was wrong? Sandra wore a look of disapproval, and Donna was close to tears. What had he said?

In fact, Donna was up and out of the room, leaving Jack and Hayley exchanging looks of bemusement.

"What did I say?" Jack asked, and then shrugged.

"What is it with men?" Sandra said simply.

"What?" No, really. What *had* he said?

"This hasn't been your mom's house since your dad died, Jack."

Jack wondered who the hell his mother-in-law was to lecture him on his own mother. He didn't say that, of course.

"It's always been yours," she said.

"Sandra—"

"And now you have Hayley. A family. This ranch is a family home." Sandra sounded wistful and ran a hand across the solid wooden table marked by years of use. "She wants you to be a family. You and Riley and Hayley."

"It's a Campbell ranch."

"You aren't a Campbell anymore, Jack," Sandra interjected. Jack crossed his arms over his chest and stared down at the slip of a Hayes talking at him like she knew anything. "You're a Campbell-Hayes."

Jack opened his mouth to talk but stopped when Hayley interrupted.

"Is that my new name? Hayley Campbell-Hayes?"

In a second any tension in the room dissolved. Hayley's expression was utterly innocent and devoid of guile.

"Yes, sweetheart," Riley said, and Jack looked over to his husband, who stood at the back door. He looked shaken, worried, and pale despite his tanned skin. And a sure sign Riley was worried or upset? He wouldn't look Jack in the eyes. "If you want it to be."

Riley might look like he'd been run over by a truck, but he was showing consideration and giving Hayley a chance to say no.

"Momma said you might want to change my name and that I should do what you say."

Riley shook his head, just as Jim had done, before he went into a crouch at his daughter's side. "We don't have to decide that now, Hayley. Your mom loved you, and her name is important. You'll always be Hayley Samuels even if you do change your name. And if you don't," he said with a soft smile as he touched the tip of her nose, "you can be a Campbell-Hayes inside."

"In my heart?"

Jack caught a fleeting glance of something in Riley. Concern, fear? He wasn't sure. What the hell had Jim talked to him about? He would ask as soon as they were alone.

Riley pressed his fingers to the middle of Hayley's chest. "In there," he said simply.

* * * * *

Eden arrived at lunchtime, and it was at that point that Jack realized just how much they'd taken on. Or rather how much had been handed to them. There was no wind of what had happened yet in the press, but Eden rightly pointed out it wouldn't be long before the story hit the papers. Her insistence they do something before people blew it out of proportion was what they were discussing.

Hayley was in her room with Sandra and Donna, and the other three took the time to try and come up with something—anything—that would keep Hayley away from prying eyes for a while.

"Her mom just died," Riley said as he argued against Eden's idea for a press conference.

"So we don't take her anywhere for a while," Eden offered. "Because if we do, there'll be photos and speculation. How about we select one journalist and do some kind of spread here at the ranch?"

Riley groaned and hid his face in his hands. Jack sympathized with him. Everything post–Jeff's murder had finally begun to settle down, and now the controversial Campbell-Hayeses needed to present a child into the mix, conceived before Riley had settled with a man. The journalists would have a field day—

"I do know someone."

Eden interrupted Jack's thoughts, and he looked at her gratefully. If Eden could get a handle on this, then it was one less thing for Riley to have to focus on. "He's my— His name is Sean Harris. Do you want me to call him?"

Riley responded with some low-pitched sound Jack couldn't make out, and so Jack agreed Eden should get this Sean Harris out to talk about interviewing the Campbell-Hayes family.

"What about school?" Eden then said.

And Jack felt his insides churn.

Where would Hayley be safe? Where could the two men keep Riley's daughter away from the shit that encircled them? Jeez, how did they stop her from becoming a spoiled brat? Jack had no real idea how much Riley was worth, but it would be so damn easy to ruin Hayley by showering her with money and gifts. When Riley mentioned she could have anything in her room, a certain level of anxiety had started to build inside him.

"There's boarding school," Jack said with only the best of intentions in his words.

Not that he really meant the idea at all.

Riley lifted his face from his hands with a horrified "No." Jack held up a hand to indicate he understood, but Riley continued. "I'm not finding out I have a daughter only to dump her in some damn boarding school!"

"A private tutor, then, at least until college?" Eden suggested.

"Yeah, and that worked so well for us," Riley snapped.

Jack hadn't been aware Riley had received the rich version of home education, and he shuddered at the thought of his other half locked in that mansion of hate while trying to learn. No wonder Riley had gone so wild at college.

"So, what do we do?" Jack tried to look supportive but might be coming across as irritable. He could hear it in his own voice.

"Other people have kids all the time." Riley knuckled his eyes. "We'll see what Hayley wants, and we'll do the right thing."

CHAPTER 9

Riley couldn't get over how grown-up Hayley appeared to be next to his niece and nephew. Losing her mother must be the hardest thing ever for an eight-year-old girl, but she was brave and strong and confident among kids she didn't know well.

Jack had lost his dad at an early age, but his mom had always been there for him. Now, Riley watched Hayley as she played with her cousins, those related by blood and through his marriage to Jack. His mom's barbecue idea had been a good one—it was an informal setting for everyone to meet Hayley and get to know her better. If only he could get his head clear of what Jim had shared with him about Hayes Oil, maybe then he could relax. Two beers in and he still wasn't relaxing.

"How have you been, Riley?"

Lisa's voice held a nervous edge, and Riley tensed when he heard it.

He wasn't avoiding talking to his dead brother's wife. After all, despite the drinking, Lisa was trying very hard to be a good mom to Luke and Annabelle. He turned to face her and felt an instant stab of pity that always accompanied every time he really took the time to look at her.

Riley had no excuse for not seeing what had happened to her at Jeff's hands. He'd just put her moods and her inappropriate come-ons down to nothing more than the alcohol talking. She looked tired but well. She had a smile on her face, and Riley pasted on a matching expression.

He evidently hadn't put enough of an effort into his smile, though, because a brief flash of uncertainty crossed her face. Shit. Covering the moment, he pulled her into a close hug, and her smile had returned when he released her.

Her blonde hair was pulled back from her face, and she was wearing jeans and a tee. Riley didn't remember ever seeing her out of a dress before, but he thought she looked so pretty. "You're looking really good," he offered with another smile.

"Seven months sober," she said proudly.

"Wow, Lisa, that's awesome." He hadn't realized how far she'd come. Why hadn't he known?

"Thank you." She blushed and dropped her gaze. "I'm not making a big thing of it." She looked up. "Y'know, with the family."

A strange mix of emotions assaulted him. First, guilt that he hadn't made more of an effort to follow what his sister-in-law was doing or, at the very least, how Luke and Annabelle were doing. Then there was a strange discomfort and a low-level embarrassment. He could pin that squarely to knowing everything he did about her.

He changed the subject. "The kids doing okay at school?" The subject of his niece and nephew was always a safe thing to ask about.

She brightened considerably, and her eyes lit up. "Annabelle is a cheerleader and is going through her first real boyfriend problems. And Luke?" She shrugged. "He hasn't taken losing his dad so well. Acting up at school— the usual teenage things, I suppose, just made worse by the fact he was a real daddy's boy."

"Can I do anything to help? I should have asked if you

needed—"

"No. Please." She reached out and touched Riley on the arm to interrupt what he was going to say. "I do need to ask you a question, though. More of a favor, I guess." She was so uncertain; it screamed from her every pore.

"Anything."

"I want you to listen to this and think about it. Talk to Jack. Agree together."

Riley glanced over at his husband, who was standing nursing a beer, watching them talk with narrowed eyes.

Lisa continued. "I want to know that, if anything happens to me, you would look out for Luke and Annabelle. I know it's a big thing to ask—especially with Hayley now—but in my will, I want to name you and Jack and Eden as guardians. Just promise me you'll think about it?"

"They're my family, Lisa. There's nothing to think about."

"Talk to Jack for me. Don't just assume he will agree."

"I will."

With her gaze fixed firmly on his, she reached up and touched his face. "You always were the best brother, Riley."

She didn't let him reply. Instead she made her way over to where Eden was dishing out salad, and Riley assumed she was going to have the same heartfelt discussion with his sister as she had done with him.

"You okay?"

Jack's voice was a welcome sound, and Riley relaxed instantly. He took the beer Jack offered him and nodded. "She wants to know if you and I and Eden would agree to become legal guardians for Luke and Annabelle if anything happened to her."

"Jeez."

Riley didn't think Jack sounded shocked or angry. If anything, he sounded overwhelmed.

"I said yes for me, and it would be enough. You don't have to say yes as well." Riley looked over to Eden and Lisa, who were hugging; he knew his sister would say yes.

"Does she not have other family she could ask?" Jack asked thoughtfully.

"Just a couple of cousins, I think. No one she's close to."

"Why me? I mean, I can see why you and Eden, but why me?"

"She knows the man you are, Jack Campbell-Hayes, the same as I do."

"Okay, then, if it's what she wants, then yes, of course she can name me."

Riley threaded his free hand through Jack's and tugged him to follow from one side of the yard to the other. "Let's go tell her, then."

* * * * *

The papers came back from the investigator on Sarah's husband, Hayley's uncle.

"He's done time for hacking...." Riley read down the paperwork. "He was some kind of computer expert who decided to embezzle from the bank he worked in. Resisted arrest and used a gun. Hence the arrest and the prison sentence."

"White-collar crime, then. He's not a murderer or a wife beater? An abuser or anything?"

"Let's say he didn't get an early release for good behavior. He did his entire sentence—five years. Finally worked his way through it and got out a few weeks back."

"So he's done his time. Why was Lexie so adamant he have nothing to do with Hayley?"

"An ex-con who failed to meet the standards for early release doesn't sound like a good role model. I still don't understand how Lexie and Sophie thought he's a threat to Hayley, but I'm sure they had their reasons."

"Okay," Jack conceded. "Maybe there's nothing we need to worry about."

Riley shrugged, and Jack could see he wasn't convinced.

"We'll see."

CHAPTER 10

"Where's Daddy?"

Now that was a leading question. Riley's phone had sounded at six, and he had left the bed with some rambling excuse about work. That was the last Jack had seen of Riley other than a hurried shower.

When Jack asked him, all Riley would say was he had paperwork to complete and calls to make for CH Consultancy. Riley was being economical with the truth—he was so damn transparent—but Jack wasn't ready to call him on it, not when they were focusing so much on getting Hayley settled.

"I'm not sure, sweetheart, but he'll be here in a minute."

They sat in companionable silence, and she continued to comb her hair in front of the large mirror in the hallway.

"It's not Dad's fault, you know," she said quietly.

"What isn't?"

Hayley didn't answer straightaway, but Jack didn't push for an answer. A good few minutes passed before she said anything else, by which time Jack had checked his watch and seen they'd need to leave in less than thirty minutes.

"He didn't know because she didn't tell him."

Her words were intense, and she startled him when she caught his hand in hers. The fingers looked so small against his, and he focused on the delicate pale skin. "Is he angry about it?"

Jack swallowed his immediate reply. *Was* Riley angry?

No. Riley was off doing fuck-knows-what for some nebulous reason he wasn't sharing with Jack. In the process he was obviously upsetting Hayley, and that wasn't right.

"No, I promise you. All your daddy wants is to find you the best school and make sure you're happy."

"Okay," she said simply.

Riley came back a few minutes later, but Jack didn't have time to call him on whatever bullshit was going on. Not when Hayley stood between them with a wide, happy smile on her face and her hand gripping Riley's.

"Want to go see your school?" Riley asked with animated enthusiasm, and Jack couldn't help but grin. "They have hamsters, you know."

God, his husband was a dork.

* * * * *

Jack was fully aware the school was—according to the research Riley had carried out—the best private girls' school they could find for Hayley. Riley had requested information, pamphlets, booklets, and prospectuses for almost twenty schools, but only this one stood out from them all.

Jack, Riley, and Hayley had sat with paperwork spread out between them. The Bryant Faraday School for Girls, just short of fifteen miles from the ranch, had ticked all the boxes. Jack liked the sports program, and as Hayley already showed signs of having her dad's height, he was adamant she would do well in high jump, long jump, sprinting, and in fact anything they offered. Riley liked the security aspects and the educational results, and Hayley was smiling as she read the pamphlets. She loved the uniform, the fact it was close to her new home, and the added evidence that there was a buddy system and a program for animal care. Because, of course, both Riley and Hayley loved the idea of hamsters in every classroom.

So there they sat, waiting on the principal, one Mrs. Olivia Andrews, who had sounded—according to Riley—very approachable on the phone. Jack had shaved that morning before Riley could get up in his face about being a cowboy, and he'd actually worn his best jeans again.

Riley, however, was too distracted to comment on anything Jack had or hadn't done. He was wearing the same suit he'd worn the day Hayley had landed in their lives, looking every inch the smooth businessman. That day seemed so long ago. Hayley really was part of their lives now, completely and utterly, even though in reality it had only been a few days. She'd laughed and giggled in the car on the way here, and even though Jack said so himself, she looked very pretty in the dress he'd pulled out of the closet for her.

They sat in uncomfortable chairs in a nondescript waiting room, and Jack wished he didn't feel like a kid waiting on some kind of cruel and unusual punishment for brawling. Or indeed any one of the hundreds of reasons he'd found his way to the principal's office when he was a child.

"Where were you this morning?" Jack asked under his breath so only Riley could hear. Riley looked straight at him, with guilt in his eyes.

"I was working," he replied just as quietly.

"Tried to find you." Jack encouraged the truth with the simple opening.

"I was on my cell by the barn. You know what reception is like in the house."

"I had to advise Hayley on her dress and hair. Does it look okay?"

Blinking, Riley turned to look at Hayley, who had her nose buried in a book. "She looks lovely," he said distractedly and pulled his cell out of his pocket.

Jack was getting closer to pissed. Riley had his phone in his hand everywhere he went. That morning, Jack had even been tempted to check the call log just to see what the hell was going on. Riley was too out of it for it to be just work. Something was happening, but Jack would have to worry about that later.

He pulled his focus back to Hayley.

"She asked me to help her with knots, and I tried to be gentle." He held his large work-scarred hands out in front of him.

Riley made a *hmm* noise under his breath but said nothing, just turned his cell over and over in his hands.

Jack decided there would be some serious conversation to be had after Hayley went to bed tonight.

"Misters Campbell-Hayes?"

Riley and Jack stood at the words and turned to face a small woman who looked like she couldn't blow over a paper tower. Gray hair and dark-rimmed glasses certainly gave her the appearance of a schoolmistress, but being so close to the floor? She couldn't be an inch over five feet, and Jack felt like a giant. God knew how Riley felt.

"I am Olivia Andrews," she introduced herself, and

then pursed her lips. "We don't tolerate cell phones at the school," she added.

Jack watched as Riley first nodded in agreement and then looked at the floor as he realized she was talking about him. He pocketed the cell, and Jack gave thanks for small mercies, wondering how Riley hadn't worn away the logo with all the rubbing he'd been doing to the poor phone.

"I apologize, ma'am." Riley used the crisp vowels of a city boy, and Jack smirked inwardly.

"Please come in." She moved into a large airy office.

The walls were hidden beneath the hundreds of photos that adorned them, alongside certificates overlaid with silver. Jack expected her to sit behind the desk set imposingly in the corner, but instead she led them to a group of comfy armchairs. The chair seemed to swallow Jack, and he struggled to sit upright, looking over to see Riley was having the same problem. Squirming without making it too obvious, he perched more toward the front. The chairs were clearly some kind of torture for parents, one way to level the playing field given her height. She forced all the tall people to fall into a sofa abyss.

"Hello, Hayley," she said.

"Hi." Hayley's voice was steady, but she inched closer to Riley and grasped his big hand.

"Your dad told me you would like to come to school here."

She was quick to respond. "Yes, ma'am."

"I have someone to take you on a quick tour of the rooms. Would that be okay?"

They heard a knock, and the door opened to reveal a

girl not much older than Hayley, dressed in the navy and red uniform Jack recognized from the prospectus.

"That would be good." Hayley seemed interested, and Jack stood up.

"Just Hayley for the time being, Mr. Campbell-Hayes. I will be giving you a separate tour after this meeting, but we need to complete some paperwork, and it is important Hayley forms her own opinions."

"Okay." Jack wanted to shrug the words off, but he felt like a naughty schoolkid again. He glanced at Riley, who was grinning at him. Great, Riley could clearly see how uncomfortable he was. Well, there was a reason he and school had never seen eye to eye. Horses never judged him for getting Fs or for his inability to sit still in classes.

They filled in the required paperwork with as much information as they had been given in the lawyer's files. With the admin stuff out of the way, it seemed they were going to get down to the gritty stuff.

"We have an experienced counseling team at Bryant, and I should imagine they would want to have regular meetings with Hayley and also with both of you. Losing a parent is a particularly traumatic experience for any young child."

"She seems…." Riley started and then looked at Jack for reassurance. "We're worried she hasn't cried or shown anything similar since she arrived to live with us."

The principal made a small note in her file. "That isn't unusual. She seems, from what you say, to be well adjusted, and the counseling will ensure she receives the right help to flourish at this school. All of this, of course, would be carried out after full consultation with the two of you."

"Thank you," Riley said.

"Our students are such that Hayley will be among other children with similar emotional needs. This is something I think is very positive." Jack and Riley nodded. "There is one other thing that's important for me to cover here."

Jack narrowed his eyes. This sounded serious.

"It is important you realize you are not unknown to the school, Mr. Campbell-Hayes." She focused her attention on Riley. "We pride ourselves on being a progressive school—"

"But you're worried about us being gay and married," Riley interrupted.

Jack didn't like the tone of Riley's voice. He sounded resigned.

"Goodness me, no," she said instantly. "Family is family. Our concern is the paparazzi that follow your story so very closely. The school is home to daughters of past governors, our elected officials, judges, and even an actor, and we have dealt with press interference before. I just need your reassurance that you will work with us to handle any problems that should arise."

"We will," Jack said, jumping in before Riley could say anything.

How the hell they were going to do that was another matter altogether. The press ate up all the gossip surrounding the Hayes family. Jack's emotions had gone from confrontational to agreeable in an instant.

But Riley was still on edge. "I can't control the papers." He leaned forward in the chair. "But I can assure you I will always have my full resources at hand should there be any issues." Olivia inclined her head in acceptance of what he said. "There's one more thing, though," he said. "I need to make sure, to know that whatever happens, as long as we can afford the fees, she can stay. Yes?"

Silence. Absolute silence as she looked at Riley with a steady gaze.

"Are you expecting a problem covering the fees?" she finally asked with a look of confusion.

"Not at all." Jack listened to Riley's instant words of reassurance, but he knew he was lying.

What the hell? Why would they ever have an issue with covering fees?

* * * * *

All the way back to the ranch, Riley alternated between best dad in the world for Hayley and shiftiest husband in the world for Jack. When they reached the ranch, Jack thought about starting a conversation, but he needed to check on Taylor. At that moment in time, he had to put his horse first. Solving the puzzle of his husband was something that would have to wait.

Riley was distant and thoughtful at dinner. His interaction with Hayley seemed normal, but his cell was never more than a hand's reach away from him. Jack tried not to feel jealous of the cell or the girl who had jumped into their lives so suddenly and with such impact.

"What's wrong, Riley?" he asked as they got ready for bed.

"Nothing. Just tired," Riley responded, shrugging.

When they lay in bed that night and Riley turned away

to sleep, it was the worst thing ever. He said it was because Hayley was down the hall, but Jack remembered back to the whole Jeff situation, and he saw the same things happening again in his husband: something big was distracting Riley, and Jack wondered if it had to do with Jim Bailey and the discussion he'd watched from the window.

Since Hayley had arrived, they'd slipped effortlessly into a routine. Of course, their sex life had taken a back seat, but it wasn't just the sex Jack missed... well, he missed the intimacy. Of course he did. And the hot sex that had burned him up every single time was a distant and fond memory, at least until Hayley went to school, but Riley had still held him in bed and not moved away.

Intellectually, Jack was aware it was Hayley's presence causing Riley's reluctance to move past a kiss. But add in the constant worry on Riley's face, and Jack was left feeling like he was missing a part of the intricate puzzle of Riley Campbell-Hayes.

Several times that evening he'd begun a conversation and left an opening for Riley to talk. But Riley, damn him, had a unique handle on Jack, and inevitably, Jack found himself talking about the ranch, the horses, or Hayley. Never about what was in Riley's head.

Tricky bastard.

And then there was the interview.

CHAPTER 11

Sean Harris arrived in jeans and a T-shirt; he drove a beat-up Toyota that had seen better days. He wasn't overly tall, maybe a few inches shorter than Jack, and he had the toned physique of a runner. With long blond hair pulled back in a ponytail and sun-kissed skin, he looked more like a surfer dude than any kind of serious journalist.

Sean waited outside the house for a good five minutes, just casting his eyes around the D, whose land spread to each horizon. Jack watched him from the kitchen and made several assumptions based on nothing but seeing a scruffy guy eyeing his land. No fucking way this was the journalist, even if Eden said it was. The dude was clearly some tabloid hack who made his living ripping the hearts out of families such as Jack's, and there was no way he was letting that happen.

His temper high, not least because Riley and Hayley had disappeared and Eden hadn't even turned up yet, Jack stalked out of the door and down the porch steps.

"Can I help you?" he snapped, thrusting his hands in his pockets and refusing the guy's outstretched hand.

"Sean Harris," the other man said. Confusion crossed his face briefly, and he dropped his hand. "Eden Hayes said you were expecting me."

"We were expecting a high-caliber journalist, not a hack."

Surfer dude's eyebrows rose in surprise, and Jack chalked that up as a success. The hack clearly hadn't been expecting someone to call him on what he was. Jack waited for the guy to turn tail but was stunned when the broadest grin crossed his face.

"These are my best jeans, dude," he said in the smile. Jack frowned at the informal tone. "Wait."

Surfer boy turned back to his car and reached into the back seat, pulling out a book and then thrusting it at Jack.

Startled, Jack took the book and glanced down at the title: *Equine Therapy*. The front was a picture of a horse not dissimilar to Solo-Cal, and Jack saw the name "Sean Harris" at the bottom.

He turned the book in his hands. "You wrote this?"

His estimation of surfer boy rose a notch. Anyone who wrote about horses must be kind of okay.

"Horses are intuitive, sensitive animals with distinctive personalities," Surfer boy—wait, *Sean*—said simply. "I grew up on a ranch back in Cali. This place reminds me of mine. You can keep the book, Mr. Campbell-Hayes."

"Jack. Call me Jack." He lifted his gaze, and instead of a guy who looked scruffy, he saw a loose-limbed cowboy with an apprehensive expression. Jack held out his hand in welcome. Finally. And Sean took it firmly. "Welcome to the D."

They were interrupted by the arrival of an irritable Eden, who'd been stuck in traffic downtown, and the return of Riley and Hayley, who'd been with the horses. Sean pulled Eden into a hug.

Jack didn't think his eyes were deceiving him when she blushed and didn't pull out of the hug so quickly. *So that's the lay of the land.*

He wondered if Riley knew.

Hayley hid behind Riley's long legs, but Sean's

judicious use of various kid-like questions, including his more-than-strange knowledge of *Glee*, had Hayley chatting happily as they stood in a loose circle.

"We probably need to take this indoors," Eden said softly.

Jack smirked inwardly at the coquettish tone of her voice. He caught Riley's quick frown and his look from Eden to Sean and back again. Jack recognized the switching on of big-brother mode; he should do—he'd used it often enough with Beth.

"Come on, big guy," he said, and nearly dragged Riley by the hand into the house.

Hayley ran in before them.

When Riley got into the kitchen, he turned. "She's flirting with him!"

"Yes, she is."

"He's scruffy."

"He's a cowboy, Ri."

Riley looked at him, blinking slowly, then realization crept over his expression, an understanding that Sean was another version of Jack. Suddenly, for an instant, in a sexy grin so hot it shattered Jack's heart and then put it back together again, he had Riley back. *His* Riley.

He stole a kiss before worried, stressed Riley returned.

"Break it up, guys." Eden's voice was filled with affection, and that set the tone for the interview.

The group took cookies, coffee, and hot chocolate into the good room—the one room that didn't have a thin layer of pervasive Texas dust covering it on regular intervals. They sat and talked for a long time, and Sean took some informal photos of Jack and Riley with Hayley sitting on

Riley's knee.

Sean knew what he was doing. He asked all the right questions and spent a special amount of time asking Hayley about her new life. He focused a little on her mom and how an eight-year-old coped with loss.

Hayley cried a little, and Jack watched as Riley pulled her in for a hug. Hayley had grief clear on her face, and it broke Jack's heart to see it, even more so when he saw a similar expression on Riley's face.

Of course Riley would grieve the loss of Lexie. He'd admitted he'd loved her in his own way, and if everything had worked the way it did in normal families, they would have maybe made a go of it. With a whole lot of ifs and maybes involved, though.

Jealousy spiked inside Jack, and he cursed the inappropriate timing of such a self-destructive emotion.

"Jack?"

Eden was saying something to him, and he tore his gaze away from his husband and back to Sean.

"Do you have anything to add, Jack?" Sean asked.

Jack had already spoken about the marriage, his love for Riley, and how Hayley fit into their lives, so he guessed he only had one thing to add.

"I can't wait for all the publicity to end so the three of us can just be a normal family. I hope people can respect our privacy."

Sean nodded at the words and then stopped the tape. He stood. "I'll get a draft of the interview to you, and you can approve the photos you want."

"Okay," Jack found himself saying. A good thing, right? Approval on a newspaper article was something the

Hayes or Campbell families were very seldom offered.

They walked Sean to the back door out of the kitchen, but Eden walked him to the car. Jack couldn't fail to notice that Sean's hand brushed Eden's as they talked with heads together.

Riley sat Hayley on the counter and boiled a kettle to make her chocolate. He was clearly not 100 percent happy with Eden and Sean.

"We don't know anything about him," Riley grumped.

Jack thought of the book in the good room and smiled. "He's an author. He wrote a book about horses."

"And that makes him okay in your eyes?"

Jack smirked at Riley's irritable assumption. "No. He just seems like a nice guy. He was brought up on a ranch in Cali; he knows horses. He seems to like Eden."

He said the last while leaning on the counter next to Hayley and observing Sean stealing the tenderest of kisses from Eden, saw Eden leaning in and gripping Sean's arms. They looked good together; affection twisted around them in an obvious bond.

"Well, I'm not sure." Riley pulled mugs down from the cupboard.

"You have to relax. It's her life, and it's your sister's choice who she falls in love with." Jack smiled, relaxed, but he was totally unprepared for what came out of Riley's mouth next.

"Don't lecture me, Jack. Jesus, man, given the way you talk to your mom, that's the pot calling the kettle black!"

Jack felt his mouth hang open. *What?* Where had that come from? Hayley was looking from him to Riley and back.

"Are you gonna argue?" she asked. She lifted her arms, and Riley picked her up and settled her on the floor. "I'm gonna go read," she said quickly. Then, with all the astuteness of an adult stuck in the middle of an impending war, she left the battlefield as quickly as she could.

"Are we?" Jack was still bemused. Even more so when Riley sighed.

"Your mom came to talk to me a couple of weeks back."

"Go on." This didn't sound good, and Jack braced himself. He'd bet this was something to do with the freaking vet.

"Neil has asked your mom to move in with him. She wanted me to tell you—"

"*No fucking way.* He lives in a one-bedroom apartment—" Sudden fear and immediate anger churned inside him like acid. The relationship between his mom and that kid scared the ever-living shit out of him.

"He bought into the practice—"

"Fuck no!" Whether the guy had a suitable home or not didn't matter one bit. He was a newly qualified equine veterinarian, and he was only three years older than Jack himself. Yes, he had a way with horses, and yes, Jack grudgingly respected what he knew, but that made no difference. Neil was not the right person to be with his mom. "He's young enough to be her son."

"Jack—"

"It's sick. He just wants her money."

"Jack—"

"I'm going to talk to him." He grabbed keys and stalked out of the kitchen, straight to Riley's SUV, next to which, Eden was still standing with Sean.

Riley was right behind him, calling him, telling him to calm down. But nothing was going to stop him. Jack had just about reached his goddamn limit, and some guy fucking with his family was the icing on the cake.

"Eden, can you stay with Hayley?" Riley called as he got into the car.

Jack didn't want his husband in the freaking car. "Fuck off, Riley," he snapped.

Every single shitty feeling inside him was building to boiling point.

"I'm coming with you. I won't let you hurt him."

"Hurt him?"

Jack was momentarily confused, and then he realized what Riley was implying. Clearly, Riley imagined Jack was going to kill Neil. And wasn't that a strong and sudden wish that spread through him like wildfire? "I'm going to talk to him. I won't kill him. Not that it's any of your business, Riley—"

"I'm going with you, Jack." Riley's tone brooked no argument.

Riley pulled his seat belt over, and Jack heard the *clunk* as it connected. Riley was evidently here to stay. Jack forced the vehicle into drive, saw Riley's wince at the grating of the gears.

"We can't all afford brand-new trucks," Jack sniped.

And suddenly every single ounce of vitriol hit Jack in an instant, all wrapped up in his fiery temper.

Fucking husband with all his money and his strong silent attitude and his cell phone and his goddamn fucking secrets. Mom being drawn in by some cheap two-bit hustler. How much more can one man take?

The roads were familiar, and all too soon the one-story veterinary practice was visible from the road.

If it was possible, Jack's temper rose another notch.

He put the car in park and stalked to the front door. Neil was in the reception area talking on the phone. He looked up and took a step back. Jack moved right into his space. Then Riley was there, pushing between them.

"Let's move this into the office," Neil was saying, but all Jack could see was red. "Jack, wait—"

Neil held his hands up in a gesture meant to placate. That just made it worse.

Jack wasn't going to hold back on this one. "If you think for *one minute* that—"

"Jack. Office. Now." Riley's voice was strident and firm.

Neil scrambled away from the wall to open his office door; once inside, he moved behind his desk.

Like having the desk there was going to stop Jack from fulfilling his mission.

Riley stood between them again, and Jack waited for him to move that single inch that would let him though to Neil.

"How much, Neil?" he growled.

"What do you mean?"

Neil was wide-eyed, but at least he was standing tall. Jack had to admire the other man just a bit for not cowering even if he had put a desk between them. Still, he didn't admire the vet enough to even consider allowing anything more permanent with his mom.

"How much money will it take to get you to leave her

alone?"

"What the hell? I don't want your money," Neil yelled.

"We can have it in your account by tomorrow."

"I love Donna—"

"Riley will pay you," Jack snapped. "So, how much do you want to—?"

"I'm not paying anything to anyone," Riley interrupted.

"I don't want her money," Neil said at the same time.

"She's twenty years older than you. What the hell else do you get out of it?"

"I love her."

Jack used his extra body mass to trip Riley forward, and when Riley released his hold on Jack to quickly balance himself, Jack took the opportunity to reach for Neil.

In seconds he had the shorter dark-haired man up against the metal filing cabinets, with his hand twisted in Neil's scrubs.

"Jack!" Riley was trying to pull him back.

"You think you're going to get to me and Riley through my mother? Is that what you want? A tap into the Hayes millions?"

"No. Jack—let me explain."

Neil pushed back and Jack stumbled. Neil wasn't dissimilar in size to himself, just a little shorter. The vet was broad and built; one final push from him and there was air between them.

Neil held out a hand.

Jack was being held back by Riley. "What else can it be?" he spat. "It has to be money. She's old enough to be your mother."

"My mother lives in San Antonio, Jack. Donna is my lover, not my mother."

"And it's just sick—"

"No. She's everything I want, Jack. She's beautiful, smart, independent, funny, and I love her. Her heart, Jack...." Neil's tone changed, and some part of it fractured Jack's temper. "She has such a good heart, and she makes me laugh. How many times do you want me to say it? It's simple: I love her."

"It's wrong." But Jack sounded less sure. He didn't feel the heat burning inside him anymore. Something in what Neil was saying was making its way through the red mist.

Riley moved between them. "Like us, then," he said simply. "We're wrong, aren't we? Two men bringing up a kid? Married to each other?"

"No—" Jack breathed deep and looked directly into Riley's hazel eyes. How could Riley say that? Was that what he thought? "There's nothing wrong with us."

Then it hit him, and in the second between one breath and the next, his anger left him and he felt nothing but shame.

"Jack?" Riley was speaking so damn quietly now.

"You love her?" Jack had to hear it from Neil again.

"I want to marry her if she'll have me." Neil winced as he said that, and Jack felt yet more guilt that the other man thought he was going to get beaten up for his words. "Wait, I have these...." He turned to the drawer behind him and pulled out a folder of papers. "I don't have anywhere near what Riley has. I probably don't have half of what you have, but there's money in the practice, and I have about a hundred thousand in the bank. Here." He thrust the papers at Jack. "You can see it all."

"Neil—"

"I'll sign a prenup," Neil continued. "I don't want anything of yours or Riley's or your mom's. I just want to be with Donna and make her happy."

Jack backed away a step, up against Riley, who supported him with a firm grip.

"I don't need to see," Jack said. "I have to go. I'm sorry."

He wasn't entirely sure what he was apologizing for. Was it the fact he'd thought the worst of his mom? Or that he'd wanted to beat Neil into a pulp? Was it that Riley had said something about them being wrong? Whatever it was, he wanted to outrun it, and he stumbled out of the room, past startled clients and out into the sunshine.

When Riley followed him into the parking lot, he grabbed the keys from Jack's hand. "I'm driving," he said. "I need a beer."

CHAPTER 12

The neon sign for Shooters was a welcome and familiar sight. It was missing the *t* and the *e*, but it still signaled the one place that leveled Jack the minute he walked through the door.

A twenty-minute drive and he had gone from scarlet with anger to a calmer temperament. Resentment still simmered below the surface, but probably due more to being angry with himself than at Neil. Jack checked out who was there, but at three in the afternoon, it really was only him, Riley, and Eddie the bartender, who was also the owner. Beers in hand, they took the corner table as usual. Riley had his cell in his other hand and was texting.

"What are you doing with that fucking cell again?" Jack asked quickly.

Riley frowned, probably at the heat in Jack's voice. "I'm just texting Eden, telling her we'll be back in a couple of hours."

"It won't take that long. One beer and we'll go back."

"Hmm." Riley was still hunched over his phone, and his phone beeped to indicate receipt of something. When he checked it, he nodded to himself, and then with a smile, sat back in his seat. "We have some time to sit and relax."

Six feet plus of Riley sprawled that way in the dented seat was a sight for sore eyes. His blond hair was longer than the last time they'd been at Shooters, only a month or so ago. It wasn't slicked back or styled to within an inch of its life anymore. Jack liked it, for reasons other than the way it looked. It gave him something to grip on to when—

Idly he looked to the left and the door to the room he'd used pre-Riley.

The door could be locked; it had a table and chairs in it, and he remembered it was always clean. Well, nearly clean. They wouldn't have lube there, but the time was well past for them to use condoms, and they could just—

"Talk to me, Jack." Riley was insistent.

"Nothing to say."

"I'm here if you need someone to listen."

Jack looked at his husband, at his tall, sinful, well-muscled body. The hazel eyes stared at him intensely. *So gorgeous.* So much time had passed since they'd done anything physical that connected them beyond hugging. He couldn't seem to get his head back into a serious discussion while he was fixated entirely on Riley and the idea of sex.

"Riley?" Jack shifted in his chair as his dick filled at the thought of Riley on his knees in front of him. Then it was easy to imagine himself on his knees, swallowing Riley to the hilt and bringing himself off to the noises he knew Riley would make. Either way he could go for.

Riley was mid-gulp, and when he looked at Jack, he didn't say anything other than, "Uh-huh."

"I want to show you something." Jack glanced back at Eddie, who met his questioning shrug with a nod.

"What?"

"Come with me." He held out his hand.

Riley stood. He kept hold of his beer, looking more than a little confused. He didn't drop Jack's hand, though, and followed him through the closed door. "What's this?" he asked.

Jack allowed him in fully and pulled the light cord. The room lit with the flickering of a bulb nearing the end of its life, and Jack looked around with eyes that weren't alcohol fogged as they had normally been in this room. It looked okay: the floor looked clean, the table looked clean. He shut the door and took the beer from Riley before backing him against the door.

"Oh." Riley huffed as Jack used his foot to widen Riley's stance, bringing his lover more to his height. He reached past him and locked the door, and as quick as that, it was on.

Every single part of Jack was in the kiss, and Riley responded with equal passion. The exhaustion, the anger, the temper, the love was all pushed between them, and the heat of them together was just right.

"Never wrong," Jack whispered against Riley's mouth.

He pulled Riley's lower lip between his teeth and then soothed the small bite. Holding tight to Riley's hands, he entwined their fingers and deepened the kiss. It had been way too long since they'd kissed past a simple good night, let alone made love, and he was so close to just bending Riley over the table and fucking him here and now—apart from the fact there was no lube.

He wouldn't, but the thought of pushing Riley flat was just one more erotic image he couldn't handle. He pressed harder, his dick firm and insistent against Riley, then he pulled back from the kiss and took in the gorgeous picture of Riley's heavily lidded eyes and pouty, swollen lips parted on a moan. Punctuating Riley's moan, Jack began an unrelenting rhythm, and his back arched as orgasm chased down his spine.

"Fuck... Jack...." Riley leaned closer for more kisses. "Please."

But Jack had other ideas. Riley whined low in his throat as Jack pulled away, but he wasn't going far. At first he simply crouched in front of Riley, releasing the hold on his hands and instead pushing his fingers into the indentation of hipbone and stretched, toned skin. Riley shifted under the hold, and there was another "Jack, please."

As slowly as he could allow himself, he unzipped Riley's pants, nearly losing it at the scent of his aroused lover. Riley was hard and needy, the tip of his dick slick with expectation, and a quick flick of Jack's tongue was enough to have Riley bucking up into his mouth. Jack pulled his lover's pants and black boxers down a little lower until he could bury himself in the darker curls at the base of his dick. Riley settled his hands on Jack's head, but there was no pressure there, just a twist of long fingers in his hair to guide him. Never to force or push.

Jack worshipped Riley with his body, with lips and tongue and fingers, pushing and sucking and pulling until incoherent ramblings spilled from his husband's mouth. He had apparently been rendered incapable of saying anything other than a string of random pleas and sprawling praise.

Jack looked up. Riley was watching him, and it was never going to be a situation where Jack could hold himself back. He flicked open his own jeans, groaning around a mouthful of Riley as he pushed material away and circled his own dick, setting up his own rhythm. *Fuck.* This was insanely hot. He was getting off by sucking his lover to completion and just listening to the noises coming from Riley's mouth.

Riley lost it first, coming hard and fast down Jack's throat. Jack heard every single word with Riley thanking him over and over.

Riley slid down the door in a crouch and stared right into Jack's eyes. Jack was so close, and he met Riley in a heated kiss. The taste of Riley between them had Jack coming seconds later, leaning against the hard expanse of Riley's warm chest and whimpering his completion against his lover. Riley simply held him, settling into a kneeling position, pulling Jack close, and holding him tight.

"Jeez," Riley murmured into his ear, and Jack just smiled and whispered words of love and want and need.

"D-do you... hot" was all Riley could say, and suddenly it was all Jack needed to hear. He had reduced Riley to a mess of fractured words and thoughts.

He had done that.

* * * * *

Hayley was waiting for them in the kitchen. She had cookies and milk and wore an expression Riley hated from the minute he walked in the door. She looked angry, terrified, and sad, all rolled into one pint-sized wall of angst. She left her drink and her cookies and walked out of the kitchen.

"I got this," Riley said, wishing he didn't have Jack's taste in his mouth and the need for Jack to be with him. Hayley was his daughter, and her witnessing them at odds with each other, while a part of life, was something he wanted to protect her from for a while.

"I like it here," she said mutinously from her perch on her bed.

Riley sat down, but there was no smile from her as his weight caused her to roll. No comment about giants and breaking beds like he'd heard every night when he tucked her in. This was serious, and he needed to pull his head away from making love with his husband at the bar and back to his daughter.

"I like having you here," he offered cautiously. "I *love* having you here," he qualified.

"You argued with Jack. I like Jack."

Riley hesitated. She liked Jack... more than him? He'd known he'd fuck this up. What did he know about having any kid, let alone a daughter?

"That's what—" *Daddies do? Parents do? Jeez.* "—we do," he finished lamely.

"Okay, I get that. Ebony's mom and dad argued a lot, and Ebony was really sad."

Riley nodded his understanding. How did he explain that when there were two men and lots of testosterone in the room—not to mention men as volatile as he and Jack—sometimes arguments could happen?

"You don't shut your door." She wouldn't meet Riley's eyes.

"I'm—we don't.... We...." Riley Campbell-Hayes, twenty-eight years old and lost for words in front of an itty-bitty girl.

"Look," she said, "Ebony's mom would shout at her dad, and he would shout back, and then there would be cuddles. And sometimes they would shut their door."

Jeez. Riley felt a blush rise from his toes to his face. "Out of the mouths of babes" or some such nonsense. "Uh-huh?"

It was the safest response he could give that didn't involve him tripping over his words. He wondered briefly if Eden was still around. Maybe this was something that should be classified as girl talk.

"You don't do that. Momma said you 'n' Jack were real happy. Like married happy, and that means you should cuddle and sometimes you need to shut the door."

"We do—"

"I haven't seen you cuddle once."

"Okay... we'll, um, cuddle," he finished helplessly.

"And shut the door?"

"Yes, we'll shut our door."

"Because I'm okay, you know."

"What?" Riley didn't mean for that to come out as blunt as it had. What did she mean she was okay?

"Momma said I would be sad, and that would be okay. I will be sad, I know. And sometimes I am sad. Sometimes I'm more than sad, and then I read her letters. But I'm okay in my room on my own."

Riley was stunned. He'd been walking on eggshells, trying not to push his relationship with Jack in her face, trying to make it all okay, and here she sat telling him he was doing it wrong. Realization smacked into him with the force of a truck.

She's right.

He opened his arms, and she clambered onto his lap and cuddled into him. He held on for dear life, choking back the emotions that threatened to burst from him, and buried his face into her neck. She smelled of apple shampoo and horses and all manner of things that reminded him of Eden.

God, the times he'd held Eden when she was little as they listened to their dad rail at their mom or when Jeff was being a particular kind of bastard to them both. He had the same love for Hayley he'd had for Eden, and it was a love that started in his heart and spread like wildfire through the rest of him.

"I love you, Hayley," he said simply.

He had only known her two weeks, but he knew she was the most precious thing to him. He, Hayley, and Jack were a family, and he needed to let Jack in.

"I love you too, Daddy."

"Jack?" he called.

If he knew Jack, then he would be loitering in the hall waiting for a sign everything was okay.

Jack peered around the door and then stepped in when Riley crooked a finger to indicate he should. He sat next to Riley and allowed himself to be pulled into a kind of odd three-way hug. Hayley just nestled in closer, and Jack inclined his head.

Riley didn't have to be told he'd done okay. He could feel Hayley's tears against his throat.

CHAPTER 13

Eden, Beth, and Donna had taken Hayley shopping, citing they had better fill her wardrobe before the article hit the press and shopping became a chore rather than an enjoyable day out.

Riley was under no illusions that once the news hit the stands, the gossip rags wouldn't pull out every single excruciating detail of what had gone on with the Hayes family last year. Hayley needed clothes, an iPod, and more books, apparently. The clothes were Eden's idea; the iPod, Beth's.

Donna was thinking along the lines of education. Hayley's uniform hung on the back of her door, waiting for Monday and her first day of school, and Donna was taking the list of what she needed to buy for then.

Hayley was visibly hopping from one foot to the other in excitement and hadn't even given her dad a backward glance as they drove off to God knew where.

Riley left Jack pacing outside Taylor's stall and took the hours to go into the office. Something wasn't going according to plan with the horse, and Jack was nearly incapable of leaving the mare. There was nothing Riley could do, and in fact it was Jack who said he should get his giant ass back to the office.

The last few weeks he'd spent at home working had pushed Riley just marginally away from having his eye on the ball, and it was good to be back sitting at his desk. Working on Sunday always felt so quiet and relaxed; there were no other staff members in the office apart from the usual front-desk security guard. He was the front face of the whole building and had control of the alarms as well as of who came in and out of the small complex that contained several different companies. It was a far cry from the tower where Hayes Oil was located, but the views were no less spectacular. Instead of the cityscape, he saw rolling hills and green grass. It suited him more.

A text came through from Eden.

Hayley is having fun.

He quickly texted a few words back and then tried to settle in to work. His latest research had led to Hayes Oil drilling speculatively in the seabed off the Texas coast, and he smiled as he read first reports from the site. The drilling was looking good for all the right mineral markers, and they had hopes oil wasn't far below.

Eighty percent of people involved in the drilling were from local towns along the coast, and Hayes Oil was being sensitive to environmental considerations, both check marks in Riley's boxes. It might not have started that way, but Riley was working hard to work within ethical guidelines. Big donations—not to bribe but to thank—were being made, and Jim and he were doing well. It wasn't going to make one hell of a lot of money, but Riley was doing what was right, and in doing so attempting to balance some of his father's and brother's wrongs.

His main phone rang, surprising him. It sounded so damn loud in the otherwise quiet working space. "Hello?"

"Hello, Mr. Campbell-Hayes, this is the front desk. There are some people here to see you."

"People?" Riley pulled his head out of his work and blinked back to the here and now.

"A Sarah and Elliot Anderson, and their lawyer, Abbot Essene."

Sarah Anderson? Quickly, he pushed the papers to one side of his desk, revealing the scribbled notes he'd made earlier. *Anderson* was the surname of Sarah's husband, the guy Lexie wanted to keep away from Hayley.

"I'll come and collect them," Riley said cautiously. "Could you please make them coffee and tell them I'm on a conference call?"

"Thank you, sir. I will."

The man at the front desk ended the call, and Riley immediately dialed an outside line. When Jim answered, Riley released a huge sigh of relief.

"Jim? Can you spare some time at the office?"

"Are you okay, son?"

"No, I think—can you come now?"

"I can be there in twenty minutes."

"Come in by the side entrance."

"What's wrong, Riley?"

"I'll let you in through the fire door at the back of the office."

"Okay." Jim paused as though maybe he wanted to ask more questions, but clearly the urgency in Riley's voice had gotten through to him. "On my way."

Riley started to pace. He couldn't sit still and think; he needed movement. His instinct was to call Jack as well, but Jack was with Taylor and all this was probably nothing more than the aunt wanting to make sure Hayley was in good hands. It must be.

Jim made it in the space of twelve minutes, and Riley didn't even want to think of the speeding tickets on Jim's license. Jim was dressed casually in denim and a tee, but he still looked every inch the lawyer. He started straight in with the questions. "What's wrong? Is it Hayley? What can I do?"

"Hayley's aunt and uncle are in reception," Riley started, his voice showing his worry. "They've brought a lawyer." He referred to the newer scribbles on his notepad. "Abbot Essene?"

"He's—" Jim paused, evidently sifting through information in his head to tell Riley what he needed to hear. "—a shark."

Riley had already run a Google search, and he could guess what Jim was going to say. "Family law, right? Adoptions, fostering, that kind of thing?"

Maybe they had the lawyer because they believed Riley was going to stop Lexie's sister having any access?

"Child placement for money. That kind of thing," Jim said sadly, and Riley straightened tall.

Well, fuck.

He walked to reception and took a few minutes to look at the three visitors from behind the safety of a Riley-sized yucca plant.

Sarah looked like her sister, with the same dark hair and slim build. But she looked older—not just the five years Riley knew there was between them, but ten or twenty. She'd scraped her dark hair back off her face, and her clothing aged her: a simple A-line skirt, sensible shoes, and a blouse. She sat nervously on the edge of her seat and stared straight ahead.

It wasn't difficult to spot the lawyer in the thousand-dollar suit, which just left Elliot Anderson. The man Lexie had hated.

Elliot was dressed simply; nothing about him screamed ex-con. No tattoos, no restless, aggressive pacing, he just sat still, opposite his wife, waiting patiently.

Elliot's hair was thick and black and pushed away from his forehead in deference to the heat. He had the look of an urbane and polished professional. The years in prison hadn't left much of a physical mark.

"My apologies," Riley said as he finally walked toward them with his hand held out in greeting.

The lawyer took his hand first, then Lexie's sister, and finally Elliot.

"Please follow me." Riley led them down the short corridor to the offices of CH Consultancy; he pushed open the door marked "Riley Campbell-Hayes."

Jim stood up, and Riley introduced him as his father. He expected Jim to correct him and add that he was a lawyer, but Jim simply raised an eyebrow. There was no sense in giving his visitors a heads-up that Riley had a lawyer present himself.

Riley pulled up enough chairs for them to sit ranged opposite his desk, and he offered them a drink. Sarah opened her mouth.

"We're fine," Elliot interrupted. He was obviously keen to get on to whatever he wanted from Riley. "We're here to make arrangements to bring Hayley back home."

Silence.

"Hayley is staying with me." Riley could be just as blunt.

Elliot pasted a condescending smile on his face. "A young man like you doesn't want to be saddled with a child. I don't know what Lexie was thinking. She was on a lot of drugs, you know."

Their lawyer was scribbling notes, and Riley stiffened at what Elliot had said. Was he implying that Lexie was some kind of drug addict? "Yes, I know. Cancer is a terrible thing," he offered instead.

Elliot narrowed his eyes. "She wasn't really in the right frame of mind to be making decisions. Was she, Sarah?"

Sarah shook her head, but Riley caught something in her expression. Was that a glimmer of defiance? Or sadness?

Jim had on his best lawyer face. "The letter my son received and the copy of the will indicated Lexie was of sound mind when she wrote that she wanted custody of Hayley to go to Riley. I'm sure you're mistaken in thinking she was less than lucid."

Elliot leaned forward in his chair, and momentarily, Riley considered that was probably Elliot's intimidating pose. Beside her husband, Sarah visibly shrank in her seat, and it reminded him of how Lisa would try to hide. Jeff's wife was outwardly strong, but in rare moments of vulnerability, she had slunk into the background as if she could disappear.

Narrowing his eyes, Riley settled back into his seat, seeing the situation for what it was. There was no love lost between husband and wife—was that what Lexie had meant? Was Elliot a bully? If he was, why was he interested in a small child? Money had to be the only motive. After all, he had been locked up on charges of embezzlement.

"You are welcome to visit any time you want," Riley

offered. "I will cover all costs for the visit, including hotel stays and transport."

Abilene was little more than three hours away, but Riley didn't want to leave anything open to chance.

"The child would be better off with her aunt," Elliot insisted.

Riley picked up on the single word "child," not "Hayley" or "Lexie's daughter" or "my niece." No, Elliot had used the generic term "child," and it sounded cold and calculating. But Elliot hadn't finished there.

"Not as part of an experiment with a man who believes he is married to another man and carries on unspeakable acts behind closed doors."

Elliot was on a roll. Despite feeling like jumping up and breaking his nose, Riley had a sudden inspiration. "I would like to talk to Sarah on my own."

"That won't be possible," Elliot said immediately.

Riley was determined to see what she would say if she was away from her domineering husband. "Nevertheless, it is what we will be doing," he said slowly.

"I'll be fine, Elliot," Sarah began.

Elliot dismissed her defense with a shake of his hand. She subsided into silence once more but sat on the edge of her seat as Jim stood and indicated the door.

"I think we should leave the father and aunt alone to talk."

He was leaving no room for maneuver, and while Elliot appeared to want to argue, he really had nothing left to say. Soon, with the attorney leaving also, only the two of them remained in the room. Riley moved around the desk and arranged a chair so he sat at a right angle to Sarah.

"Don't let him do this," Sarah breathed, and looked over her shoulder, clearly scared Elliot was going to rush in at that very moment.

"Do what?"

"He doesn't want Hayley. He just wants control of whatever trust fund you establish for her."

"I thought it might be that," he offered gently.

"Lexie never had a single bad word to say about you, Mr. Campbell-Hayes. She said she thought you had grown up well and Hayley would be happy with you."

"Riley, please."

"Riley, then."

They sat in silence a moment longer.

Riley tried to be as gentle as he could. "He's not long out of prison. Is that what scares you?"

"No." Sarah looked like she was about to cry. In that instant, with her defenses lowered, Riley could see Lexie in her eyes. "It scares me I waited this long for him to come home and then realized I want to leave him."

"I have the money to help you—"

"It's not about money, Mr.—Riley. It's having the strength to leave him. All those years he was behind bars, I could stay married, and it didn't matter. But now he's back. He's not the same man. I mean… he is the same. He's still overbearing, but he has nightmares. I want him to get help, but he's fixated on Hayley and the money he knows she'll have."

"Thank you for your honesty." Riley so wanted to be the grown-up here. He couldn't, though, when all he wanted to do was go home and grab Hayley and never let her go.

"I won't fight for custody. I only came to make sure you understood this is not my idea or my wish. I won't bring Hayley into our house, no matter what Elliot wants to do."

"But you'll be okay? With Elliot?"

"I don't think he's a bad man. He just sees what others have and wants it all. I know who I married," she finished cryptically. Then she stood, left the room, and pulled the door closed behind her.

For a second, Riley waited. He needed to take everything in; he hoped that she would somehow break free from Elliot and make a stand.

The door burst open, and Elliot was there with a taut, furious expression on his face. "I don't know what the fuck you said to her," he spat, "but one way or another, we'll get what is ours."

"Mr. Anderson—"

"Fucking fags." Elliot spun on his heel and stormed out of the office and down the corridor.

Riley followed him to the end of the corridor to make sure he really left the building. Sarah stood with the lawyer and just shook her head. Lowering an argument to personal insults was a sign of desperation, and Riley bit back the need to shout something back. He could rise above this.

Jim stood quietly. The other attorney spoke. "My client will accept an out-of-court settlement in lieu of suing for custody," he said plainly.

Riley stiffened.

"Who is your client?" Jim asked just as plainly.

"Mr. Elliot Anderson."

Riley barked out a laugh and Jim shot him a censorious look.

"Please feel free to file the paperwork for our consideration," Jim said.

Avarice shot into the other lawyer's eyes, and Riley wondered what percentage of a final settlement he would receive. Sarah followed the lawyer out, and at the last moment, turned and shot a grateful smile in their direction.

Riley kind of liked Lexie's sister. Then, when everyone had gone and it was just Riley and Jim left, he pulled two beers from the fridge and passed one over. After taking a long slug from his own bottle, he sat down on the nearest chair.

"They don't have a hope in hell, son. The only connection there is Sarah, and even then, historically, a sibling relationship does not outweigh a parental one."

"What about"—Riley wasn't sure how to word it, so instead it came out like a careless comment—"the whole, y'know, gay thing."

Jim lifted the beer and swallowed. He was evidently delaying what he wanted to say, and Riley's stomach sank. If it came to a choice... if he had to choose between Jack and Hayley... God....

"Two people. Married. In love. Financially secure. A strong family network, and two lawyers in the family? They haven't got a snowball's chance in hell of getting anything from you. Hayley is loved and wanted, and my granddaughter is staying where she damn well is now."

Jim had a passion in his eyes that made Riley smile. He didn't think about what he said next and wasn't surprised to hear himself say, "Thanks, Dad."

CHAPTER 14

"There's no going back from this once we decide to go to press," Jack passed the draft interview and photos to Riley, then sat back in the seat with a bottle in his hand.

His serious expression unnerved Riley. "All we have to do is sign off on this, and that's it?" He wasn't really questioning the article; he just wanted to be sure.

Jack stared down at the words Sean had written. "It's good," he said simply. "It doesn't dramatize Lexie's death, or belittle the loss. It doesn't mention Sarah or her idiot of a husband, and it paints us in a good light." He traced his fingers over the headline: "The Campbell-Hayes Family Welcome Riley's Daughter, Hayley, into Their Lives," and stretched out in the chair.

It was past midnight, and Sean had only left half an hour before. He had arrived at seven with Eden, and there was an open affection between the two of them that no one could miss. Eden was happy, and Riley tried really hard to tamp down a big brother's instinct to maim. Jack, the bastard, knew what he'd been going through, but his idea of helping was to grin inanely and wink. *Fucker.*

Hayley was long since in bed, and it was just the two of them. His cell had been mercifully silent this evening. Even though it was in his pocket, just in case, they'd left him alone.

After what had happened in the office the day before, how could he even think of keeping a secret from the man who was his other half? Jack would understand. *Please God, let Jack understand.*

Jack would listen, and he wouldn't think back to the old Riley Hayes; he would trust the new Riley would be telling the truth.

Knowing he should be sharing everything with Jack was eating away at him. Ever since the day Jim had pulled him to one side and told him what Jeff had done, Riley had debated coming clean with Jack. But they had Hayley, and Jack was experiencing problems with Taylor, and—it was all excuses, really. At the end of things, he was scared all the way to his core. It would probably be best if he waited to tell Jack until after everything was settled with Hayley. Or until—Shit, he just needed to tell Jack everything.

Not tonight, though. He would cross that particular bridge another day.

Which was why he was so damn surprised when he suddenly blurted the whole mess in one long piece of verbal overload.

"Jack, there's something I need to talk to you about. It's important. Jim said the Office of Inspector General was investigating this guy, Abraham Jenkins. They say he used inside knowledge of government contracts to assist oil companies like Hayes Oil in gaining an advantage over other companies when bidding."

Jack sat there with his mouth wide open.

Riley inhaled deeply. *Shit. How did all that come out so clearly and on one single breath?*

"Like this Jenkins gave Hayes Oil a heads-up," Jack summarized.

It wasn't unknown. Riley had intimate knowledge that it wasn't what you knew but who you knew that drove the oil machine.

"Yeah, in 2007—" He paused. He had to try to remember this right if it was going to make sense. "—an exploration and contracts management subsidiary of Hayes Oil, called Elementrix, paid Jenkins around $1.2 million."

"And this was Jeff finding ways to get contracts first? Is this what has been keeping you on the cell? It's too late for people to be worrying about it now; Jeff's dead." Riley was uncomfortable, and Jack picked up on it immediately. He leaned forward in his chair and rested his elbows on the table. "What is it, Riley?"

"It isn't Jeff's name on the paperwork."

"Gerald, then?"

"Elementrix was mine, Jack, and my signature is on the checks." He dropped the bombshell and waited for Jack to hit the roof—shout at him or rail at him.

Jack didn't. He simply shrugged, then rested his chin on his steepled fingers. "How did Jeff do it? Did he forge your signature?"

Overwhelming relief flooded Riley at Jack's casual acceptance that Riley had nothing to do with it. He hadn't realized how weighed down he'd been by the possibility Jack might not understand. "He must have. I know I didn't do it."

"And the OIG? What do they say?"

"They said they will put it through handwriting analysis, the whole thing, but they aren't looking at me, really. They wanted to make me aware of what had been happening at Hayes Oil. Like I didn't know what my brother and Gerald were capable of. The OIG also suggested this may well unearth a whole area of shady shit Jeff had hidden. All the payments were signed off by me as director of Elementrix, and because the exploration contracts side of Hayes was mine, he could hide his involvement. But I never had anything to do with budgets and accounts."

"What about audits? Wouldn't they pick up the anomaly? They would have told you."

Riley looked uncomfortable. "I didn't take the time to know what was happening, Jack. I never did. To anyone who looks, it's Riley Hayes who broke the law. It doesn't stop there, though." He stopped and closed his eyes briefly, anything not to see Jack's disappointment or horror. "It's bigger than Jenkins. Two people involved in this case have died in suspicious circumstances. It looks as if whoever was forging my signature from Hayes Oil was involved in something far larger.

"They think it was Jeff. All evidence points to him and Gerald."

"Suspicious deaths? Shit. What the hell was your family doing?"

"I'm sorry, Jack." Riley's voice was small and tired.

"So are they trying to pin this on you now? Do we need to get lawyers involved? I can get Josh here."

"They want me to help them. Something about wearing a wire and getting close to this Jenkins guy. I can't get this out of my head, Jack. What did Jeff do? What the hell am I in the middle of? Why would you even want to go through any more shit with my family? And jeez, what if you think it was me all along?"

To his credit, Jack didn't interrupt once. If anything, a

veil appeared to have lifted from his eyes, and understanding dawned in their depths. "This is what has been tying you in knots these last few weeks. You didn't think I'd believe you had nothing to do with it?"

"After the way we met, why would you? After I blackmailed you?"

Jack raised his eyebrows at the words. "Riley—"

"No," Riley said tiredly. "I never really thought you would think it was me. I trusted you would know I didn't have any more secrets."

"So, what do we do now?"

Riley was never more thankful to hear the heavy emphasis on *we*. "The OIG have pulled in the FBI."

"Jeez, it's letter hell."

Jack snorted, but Riley didn't crack a smile.

"Apparently this whole thing is one huge conspiracy, and it goes a hell of a lot deeper than just some signed paperwork. They want me to approach Jenkins with an offer, give him some shit about how I need to recoup money from Jeff's mismanagement, and get Jenkins to meet me while I'm wearing a wire."

"When is this happening?"

"I don't know. They're feeding the bull to him now, setting up the whole line on contracts."

"And all you're doing is meeting him?"

"Wired."

"Wired. Okay. And you haven't told me this because…?" Jack raised an eyebrow to punctuate the question.

Riley looked at his husband, searching for evidence he was pissed or disappointed or any of a hundred different things that could mean Riley had fucked up again.

"I don't want anything to do with what Jeff did. I'm still feeling—" For a few moments, he couldn't find the right word. "—ashamed? Yeah, I feel ashamed at some of the shit he pulled." He watched Jack relax. That was definitely the right thing to have said, and who said he shouldn't just tell the truth? "I have to pretend like I'm not the person I am, and I'm no more than…." He couldn't finish the sentence. Instead, he shrugged.

"A criminal."

"If they don't get him and they decide to come after me…. Fuck, Jack." Riley felt a million different kinds of hate and resentment building inside him, and it all threatened to spill out. Jack held out a hand across the table, and Riley gripped it hard. "They don't have to have any evidence to undermine the new work I'm doing. And they could bring shit down on this family by dragging my name in the dirt."

"You didn't do anything. It's not your signature on those papers. You could step away from what they're asking you to do now, and they would have nothing."

"I can't do that to Hayley. I can't leave this hanging over us. They said, if I do what they ask of me, I wouldn't be named anywhere and the Hayes name would be kept out of it."

"Okay, so, you're just acting. Doing a good thing," Jack concluded, summing up the whole mess with an extra shrug and a yawn. After all his weeks of worrying, Riley couldn't believe Jack was this laid-back about the whole thing. "Come on. We'll sleep now, and then talk in the morning."

Riley followed him out of the kitchen and toward the back of the house. They paused outside Hayley's room, and he concentrated on the small lump under the quilt, but he couldn't make out which way her head faced and which were her feet. She slept just like he did: curled under the quilt and so deeply asleep it was as though she would never wake up. He couldn't go in and kiss her goodnight because she was buried so deep.

Jack tugged him from the doorway, and with a smile, Riley allowed Jack to lead him to the bedroom.

"Can we shut the door tonight?" Jack asked softly.

"Please."

CHAPTER 15

The pony arrived two days before Hayley's birthday, and Jack spent a long time making sure she was equipped with all the right "horsey things." Well, that was what Riley called them. He had actually glazed over when Jack stood and explained the bloodline for this new, smaller version of Taylor and Solo. He zoned out somewhere between *temperament*, *pinto*, *skewbald*, and *tobiano*.

"It's kind of brown and white," Riley teased. He loved it when Jack got all up in his face with horse facts and figures and never failed to find a place to rag on his husband.

"Sorrel, Riley. A sorrel and white."

"Is it a girl or a boy?" Riley added innocently. Jack looked at him pointedly, and Riley smiled.

"It's a gelding."

His husband looked so proud and excited about the pony he had found for Hayley, and Riley just about fell in love with the man all over again. Hayley was still sleeping and Donna was at Neil's, which meant it was just the two of them leaning on a fence, watching Hayley's pretty pony investigate his surroundings. Riley turned with his back to the pony and leaned on the fencing, with one foot up on a railing. He considered Jack as he talked on and on about Taylor and the upcoming foaling. There was such passion in this cowboy, for his horses, for his ranch, and for life. He never did anything by half, and he had been so damn understanding about Hayley and the Hayes Oil mess.

"I love you." Riley interrupted whatever Jack had been

saying, and for a second, Jack just stared at him.

"Yeah?" he finally asked, and took those few steps until he pressed close to Riley's side. "What did I do to deserve you saying that, Het-boy?"

It was Jack's usual way to lighten any intense situation with humor. But this wasn't *that* time. Riley had things to say, and saying them out here on D land, with the house behind them and acres of land beyond, seemed just the right thing to do.

"For Hayley," Riley began. He reached out and curved his hand around Jack's face, the skin prickly and rough with stubble. Riley noticed a few lines around his eyes. Tough Texan-sun-toned skin and eyes a deep, clear sky blue made one sexy package. Jack pressed against Riley's palm and didn't drop his gaze. "I love you for Hayley. You're doing this for her and taking it so seriously. I love that you're going to teach her to ride properly so she will be safe, and I love that you give her and me the time to be *us*."

"Riley—"

"No, wait. I love that you trusted me about those contracts and didn't immediately think I had anything to do with it. Despite our past, you trusted me." He stopped briefly; he had so much more to say. "I love the coffee you make me and the way you don't fight me sprawling and taking up more than half the bed. I love the noises you make when you lose it inside me. I love the way you close your eyes when we kiss, and the wonder I see there when you open them."

"Oh." Jack raised his eyebrows. "That's kind of an intense thing to lay on a guy at six in the morning."

Riley had a second of worry that this was Jack's way of escaping the intensity of what he'd said. That thought only lasted a second as Jack leaned in and gripped handfuls of Riley's shirt.

"I love that even before you knew Hayley was yours, you were her daddy," Jack said simply. "And I love you want to make things right at Hayes Oil, but I hate that you were worried I wouldn't think either was good—"

"Jack—"

"But I know why you thought those things. I understand. Okay?"

Jack was asking far more than just a response to his words. He wanted Riley to know he would always acknowledge his fears and hopes as being real.

Riley dropped his hand and instead put both arms around him and held him close. He smelled of the shower gel they used and the early-morning air. Riley inhaled deeply.

He smells like home.

"Daddy!"

Hayley's voice was coming nearer, and Riley released his hold on Jack. They exchanged goofy grins.

"Daddy! Is Red awake?"

It had been difficult to keep the pony a secret, and Jack had been way too excited not to tell her the minute Red had arrived a few days before.

Getting Hayley to sleep had been near impossible last night, and Riley was amused that she'd slept so long this morning, it being her actual birthday. She reached them. In a smooth move, Jack caught her and swung her up on the top rail of the fence. She scrambled to sit, and suddenly it was the three of them looking at the new pony.

Hayley was visibly vibrating with excitement. "Pappa, he really is so beautiful."

Riley looked at her. That was a new one, calling him Pappa when he was normally Daddy.

"I know he is. Jack chose well, didn't he?" Riley smiled at her as she turned to face him.

"Yeah, he did, but I'm talking to Jack, Daddy, not you. He's Pappa."

Riley's heart nearly exploded in his chest. This moment right here, looking at Red, standing with the man he loved, and listening to his daughter call his husband Pappa... this was way past incredible.

* * * * *

Hayley's birthday passed without a hitch. Riley wanted to buy every single toy and game he could find. He wanted her to have everything. Common sense slapped him in the face, and with Red saddled and waiting, they really had given her the best birthday ever. He worried she would be sad as it was her first birthday without her mom. So there was an apprehension building inside him as to how the hell he was going to deal with it.

In the end, he just held her when she cried.

She had disappeared from the huge birthday spread Donna had prepared and the chaos of two families fighting for food and space in the small kitchen. It was all loud and chaotic, filled with laughter and teasing and love.

When Riley found her, she was with Red. A coloring book and some pens that Eden had given her lay out on the grass. It was a book full of horse outlines, and she'd just stared at it for a long while. No one else but Riley seemed to notice.

Hayley was on her tummy in the grass, the book open in front of her and the pens in disarray around her, but she wasn't coloring now. Instead she was staring ahead with her chin resting on her crossed arms. Her little legs were bent at the knee, and she was swinging them idly. Riley crouched next to her.

"Hey, Hayley," he said gently.

She glanced sideways at him. He could see she had been crying; her intense brown eyes were red-rimmed. He sat the rest of the way down and hesitated. Maybe she needed some alone time? Who was he to think he could understand her or make things better for her? He wasn't arrogant enough to imagine for one minute that she needed him at this time.

"'M just a bit sad," she half whispered. "I'm sorry."

"Why are you sorry?"

"I know I shouldn't be sad."

"You have every reason to be sad, sweetheart."

"But I got a pony. Ebony doesn't have a pony. So I gotta be happy."

Riley waited before he answered. Ebony was Hayley's friend and maybe he should think of bringing Ebony here for a visit. Hayley had been ripped from everything she knew to be placed with him. Damn—why hadn't he thought of that for her birthday? He never even considered inviting Ebony or Sarah or Aunt Sophie. And he called himself a dad?

"Nope. You don't have to be happy, baby. You can be

as sad as you want to be about your momma."

Wait, should he be saying that? Hell, maybe he should be telling her about how her momma was in a better place, looking down from heaven, or that she was a star or something. Jeez…. He really had to hit the Internet when he got his next time alone.

Hayley sat up and scrubbed her eyes. "Your daddy is dead. Aunty Eden told me. And your brother… he's dead too."

"Yes, they are."

"Do you cry?"

Christ. A leading question if ever he'd heard one. Did he cry? God, no. Not for them, anyway. He had cried for what they'd done to Donna and Jack and Beth, but for himself? He didn't miss either Gerald or Jeff and wondered if he ever would. It didn't matter that his dad had made some grandiose gesture to make amends; the damage had been done.

Riley didn't want to lie to Hayley. Lying to kids was wrong—that much he knew from his limited knowledge of child psychology. It was best to try to stick to the truth.

"I get sad," he said simply.

The truth. In among the hate and the denial and the disgust resided a kernel of sadness. Of course, it was wrapped in his own pity party for one, snuggled right next to self-loathing, but it was there.

Hayley climbed onto his lap, and instinctively he caught her and settled her close. Her small hands wrapped around his neck, and she was clinging, secure in his hold. She was crying again, noisy sobs that shook her frame, and all he could do was hold her and hope to hell he was doing the right thing.

Jack found them a little later, and by that time tears had turned to talking, and Riley even felt like he might have some control of the situation.

"Hey, guys," Jack said softly, and Riley caught his concerned expression. There were questions in the blue depths of his eyes, but Riley didn't even know where to begin to answer.

"Hi, Pappa." Hayley's voice was muffled against Riley's chest.

"You okay out here?"

"We're fine," Riley began. "Aren't we, Hayley?" He hesitated to hear a response, just in case she wasn't fine now.

She turned in his hold and looked up at Jack, and Riley could only imagine the puppy expression she was turning full force on her Pappa.

"Is it time to do riding yet?" she asked hopefully.

Jack smiled and held out a hand to help them both stand.

"Sure is, li'l lady," he drawled in his best cowboy. "Cake first, then ridin'."

She skipped ahead to the house, and Riley had one thing to say. "I don't know if I can do this right," he said miserably.

"Yes, *we* can," Jack replied, with a whole lot of emphasis on the *we*.

* * * * *

To see his daughter on Red, making all the rookie

mistakes of a first-time rider, was just really an excuse to stare at Jack as he led the pony and its precious passenger around the paddock. Hayley wasn't talking; she had her lower lip caught in her teeth and was concentrating about as hard as Riley had ever seen her. Jack was chatting about something, probably guidance on how to sit and guide Red to do what she wanted him to.

Riley pulled out his phone and snapped a few pictures.

"She's so beautiful up there," Jim began conversationally.

"She is."

"A natural," he added. Riley knew Jim was biased, just as he and Jack were. "I left the papers you need to sign in an envelope in the kitchen."

Riley looked at his dad with confusion. "That was quick. Shouldn't there be more... I don't know, difficulty?"

"Not at all. You knew what you wanted, and I just need your signature to transfer the money."

"Am I doing the right thing?"

"You're a rich man, Riley. Most rich men have trusts set up for their children."

"What if...?" How the hell was he going to explain the things that haunted him when he was trying to sleep? "What if we hadn't had all that money, if we had been a normal family?"

"Are you thinking about Jeff specifically?"

"Not just him, but Gerald and what he was like, and my mom, and what happened to you. All the things that were so wrong."

"Hey, Daddy, Grandpa! Look at me!"

Red didn't even react to the shout, bless him. He just kept on walking. When Jack said the pony was good with children, he hadn't been wrong. Hayley was close and looked like she wanted to wave but couldn't let go of the death hold she had on the reins. Riley grinned over at her and waved, as did Jim. Jack quirked a smile at them both and set off on another circle of the small training paddock.

Jim continued. "Quite apart from everything else, son, there was something very wrong with Jeff. He had evil inside of him, so ingrained it wouldn't have mattered if your family was a pastor's family from Ohio."

"How much is in the trust?"

"About seventeen million, give or take a few thousand."

"And it's safe?"

"All in Hayley's name and locked for her twenty-fifth birthday. Eden, Beth, Steve, and Josh are trustees, as you asked."

Riley nodded. The money was nearly three-quarters of everything he owned after investing in his consultancy, and now it couldn't be touched by him or by anyone else. He trusted Eden with his life and knew she would show Hayley how to enjoy the money. Beth would show Hayley how to be a good person and use the money to help others. Steve would show her how to trust and have fun in life while still being sensible. Josh was strong and stable, a family man. If something happened to Riley and Jack, then Riley couldn't wish for four better influences for his daughter.

They'd decided they would like Eden to be her guardian, and when they'd asked her, she'd agreed instantly.

"What about the other stuff? I want Jack to officially adopt."

"It's not looking good, son. We know state law allows single GLBT adoption, which in your case is irrelevant anyway as you are her father. There was a case not long ago where a stepfather couldn't adopt without the express permission of the mother, but that is the closest I've come to precedent. Given Lexie is deceased, she can't give permission, so there's a gray area there. Christ knows what a judge would drum up if pushed. Gay adoption is a political hot potato, and it's entirely up to you if you want to fight this."

Riley's chest tightened. "I have to know she will be Jack's if anything happens to me. I don't want her going to Sarah and Elliot."

"I'm doing my best to find a legal solution."

"And what if we don't find one?"

"Riley, if anything happens to you, we can tie this up in court until she reaches an age she is deemed capable of deciding for herself. But there is one other option."

"Which is?"

"Move to another state where the gay adoption petition is legal."

Riley didn't even hesitate. "I couldn't make Jack leave the D."

"Just a thought. Okay?"

"Thank you for doing this for us. I'll talk to Jack."

"Well, we need to call in the family law attorney dealing with all of this, but at least we have some idea of what we want here."

"Daddy! Grandpa!"

Jack was helping Hayley off the horse, and as soon as her feet hit the ground, she was off running.

"Hayley, wait," Jack said firmly. She spun on her heel. "You can't just run off. We need to be looking after Red now."

Riley waited for the complaining, but instead his daughter just threw him a bright, wide grin and trotted back to Jack.

"Coming, Pappa." Together, the two of them led Red out of the gate and off to the stable.

"Jack's good with her," Jim commented. As Sandra joined them at the fence, he placed a hand over her shoulders.

"She called him Pappa," Sandra said.

"Yeah," Riley said. "It's cool."

CHAPTER 16

The car that drove up to the D the next morning was, Jack imagined, some kind of FBI car: a dark sedan with blacked-out windows so there was no way of knowing who was inside. An older, gray-haired guy wearing a dark suit and the shiniest black patent shoes Jack had ever seen on a ranch climbed from the passenger seat. "I'm looking for Riley Campbell-Hayes." He stood with his feet apart, his arms crossed over his chest.

"Can I ask who you are?" Jack planted his feet firmly. Feds on his land were not going to intimidate him.

They stood in a battle of wills, eyeball to eyeball until a cough separated them.

"Agent Jones, I assume?" Riley jumped down the last two steps and offered a hand to the new guy.

"Mr. Campbell-Hayes?" The agent inclined his head.

"Call me Riley. This is my husband, Jack."

Jack narrowed his eyes at the casual introduction.

"I wonder if we could go somewhere to talk," the agent said.

"We have coffee," Riley suggested, then turned to Jack. "We can use the good room, yeah?"

Jack hesitated to answer. He wasn't sure he wanted Riley off in another room with someone who was nothing more than a high-level cop who appeared armed.

"Jack is going to sit in on this," Riley insisted.

To give him his due, the agent didn't twitch a muscle at that.

Riley started rambling. "My daughter is at school…."

Jack listened to him with half an ear. He indicated with a hand gesture that Agent Jones should precede him into the house, and after a few seconds of posturing, the man did as Jack wanted him to. Clearly, he didn't like having his back to strangers. Well, neither did Jack. Twenty years of bar fights had taught him one thing—you couldn't defend yourself if you couldn't see your opponent. That was one reason why Jack was so damn good at bar fights, if he said so himself.

They settled in the room. Three coffees in mugs stood on the table and an unopened box lay between them. Agent Jones opened it and pulled out a Rolex very similar to the watch Riley owned, all flash and platinum.

"There's no need for visible wires. There's a tracker inside the mechanics of the watch and a speech recorder. All you need to do is press the dial here—" Jones leaned forward and indicated the side of the Rolex. "—then get him talking."

"About what, exactly?" Jack asked as Riley didn't seem inclined to do so.

"Two people have died, son," Jones began, and Jack bristled at the condescending tone. "We have no leads other than the signatures of Jenkins, Jeff Hayes, and of course Riley, which he alleges isn't his."

"It isn't his." Jack moved forward threateningly in his chair, and the tension inside him promised to jump out at any moment.

The agent didn't even blink. Evidently he was semi-threatened by cowboys every day, and it didn't move him one bit. "We are fully aware of what is and isn't Riley's involvement in this case," the agent said, dismissing Jack with nothing more than an icy half-smile. "We have set up the meet for today. Midday at Cassis Alessandro." The agent named one of the most expensive, and equally discreet, restaurants in Dallas. "Get him talking about Jeff, about how you need to travel the same path. Get names, anything, but get specific references to the documents and agreements from 2007."

"I understand," Riley said. He loosened his own watch and dropped it to the table. A timepiece worth thousands of dollars sat between three chipped coffee mugs. At that moment, Jack realized he'd never felt so much dread pour through him. He looked on as Riley picked up the other watch and placed it on his wrist. He couldn't see much difference between the two.

"Nothing is going to happen there, Jack. I'm just going to talk."

Emotions trickled through Jack that he didn't want to begin to identify—fear, resignation, and the overwhelming desire to push Riley into a room and lock the door on him.

"He's talking, recording, and that's it? What then?"

"He pays the check and leaves. There will be surveillance on him at all times, but we don't think Jenkins is involved directly with the murders."

"You don't *think*?" Jack stood and began to pace. "You don't *think* he's involved with the murders?"

"Jack." Riley stood to join him. "All I have to do is a bit of acting, okay? They're recording from the watch, probably to some van outside. It's a quick in and out, and it will give them somewhere else to look for criminals away from Hayes Oil."

"We can still just check the documents they say you

signed against your own handwriting—"

"It's gone past that. They're not forcing or blackmailing me. I want to do this. I want to close down all the doors that link me to back then."

"Just come home to me and Hayley safe. Promise me you will get your ass straight home," Jack demanded.

He completely ignored the third man in the room. As far as he was concerned, it was always him and Riley against the world.

As though aware of Jack's focus on Riley and the two men's exclusion of him, Agent Jones cleared his throat and said, "I'm going now. If you have any questions you can call me."

He handed a card to Jack and one to Riley and abruptly left.

All Jack wanted to do was kiss Riley, brand him, keep him hogtied to the bed.

He settled for drawing him closer and just keeping it to the kissing.

* * * * *

The restaurant was anticlimactic. Riley didn't know what he had been expecting, but it certainly wasn't the small man in a suit, who looked more like an accountant than a master criminal. In fact, that was exactly what he turned out to be—just an accountant of sorts. He made Riley promises he had apparently made to Jeff before. The accountant didn't seem to wonder for one minute whether Riley was anything but who he claimed to be—someone who needed access to contracts and funds, unable to go about it down the legitimate route.

"I can get you forty-eight hours on everyone else for new contracts," the man said with a self-satisfied grin. He leaned back in his chair, twirling a glass of port. "Jeff always came to me. I wouldn't even like to list the billions Hayes Oil made off my intelligence information."

"How do you get the information, then?" Riley attempted to inject innocent enthusiasm into his voice; making the movement as natural as he could, he placed his hands on the table so the watch wouldn't miss a single word.

Jenkins was nearly preening, and he moved forward in a posture that screamed he was going to share secrets. "If I told you, I'd have to shoot you." He smirked, and Riley had never been closer to punching someone in the face than at that moment. "In all seriousness, though—" Jenkins sat back and looked at him with an expression Riley could only describe as sly. "—I had a good percentage with your brother." He shook his head slowly and raised his glass. "He'll be missed." Riley gritted his teeth and lifted his own crystal tumbler of iced water in mock salute. "It was just a shame the McAllisters got… well, you know."

Riley's stomach clenched. Was that a name he should know? Maybe he should go along with this.

"A terrible situation," he offered carefully.

"It wasn't my idea, you know," Jenkins pointed out, the fine wines and port obviously playing havoc with his ability to be discreet. "Someone higher than me ordered the hit. I must admit, I was more than a little put out not to have been included in the negotiations."

"With McAllister?"

"Yes. I knew him well, told them he would have everything they needed at the estate."

"His estate?" Riley widened his eyes in mock surprise. He didn't have one iota of an idea what the fuck this accountant guy was talking about. He couldn't overplay his hand here.

"Martha's Vineyard. I went there a lot, you know. Was very close to his wife, if you know what I mean."

At that point, Riley wondered if Jenkins was going to wink. When, in fact, Jenkins *did* wink, a bubble of hysterical amusement attempted to rise in Riley, but he pushed it down ruthlessly as Jenkins carried on spilling his secrets.

"So all that time he had what they wanted, but hell if they're going to get it now he's dead."

"Hmm," Riley encouraged.

Jenkins's cell sounded for a received text and he looked down at the flashing screen. Riley noticed a quick spark of an expression—fear?—and then it disappeared as quickly as it had appeared. Jenkins stood. Clearly, Riley was getting the check for the dinner, as suddenly Jenkins seemed very keen to leave.

"You'll be hearing from me."

Which wasn't going to happen, because when Riley exited the restaurant some five minutes later, Jenkins was dead on the sidewalk, with a bullet directly between his eyes and his brains splattered on the wall behind. A huddle of people clustered around the body.

Paramedics arrived, and Riley backed away. He had to get away from there before anyone questioned who

Jenkins had been with. There was no way he wanted to deal with local cops; he'd let the Feds sort this out.

In shock, he drove home. The welcome sight of the DD sign as he passed under it served as a barrier against the horror of what he'd just seen. His cell rang as he climbed out of his car, and he answered the call.

"We have the shooter. And a new lead in the McAllister murders. Job well done" was all Agent Jones had to say.

"You knew he was going to get shot?"

"Not exactly, though we suspected someone wanted him dead, and assumed he did as well. He knew too much, and that's probably the reason he's been in hiding. We knew the risks, but we needed to know who ordered the hits on the McAllisters, and why, and what names Jenkins might throw out to you in the conversation."

"That's fucking cold."

"We had to pull him out of hiding, and the lure of money and the Hayes name was enough."

"You used me."

"I wouldn't go that far, Riley. We had no choice. You were the only draw big enough. As I said, we have the shooter—"

"What if I had been standing next to him?"

"It was a precision shooting—"

"What the fuck—"

"Goodbye, Mr. Hayes."

"*Campbell*-Hayes, asshole!" Riley shouted, but he was talking to nothing but thin air.

Alone in the ranch house, he pulled off the suit and dropped it straight into the garbage. The lot: jacket, pants, shirt, and tie. He scrabbled to unhook the watch and went into the bedroom to throw it onto the bedside cabinet, then thought twice in case he had depressed the Record button. Instead he placed it carefully on a side table, face up, making sure it was in the off position. Fucking thing.

Part of him wished he felt grief at what had happened to Jenkins, but all he actually felt was anger. He'd been used, and he could have freaking died out there today.

Hayley wasn't due home for a while. He'd asked Eden to pick her up from school, and she'd said she would be taking Hayley "girly shopping."

Where the hell was Jack? He needed Jack. He needed a bar fight, or just a fight, or hard, mindless sex.

"I heard the car." Jack's voice made him spin to face his husband at the bedroom door. "Was it…. Did it go okay?"

Jack didn't look good himself.

"Okay." Riley instantly attempted to reassure Jack, hoping he couldn't tell Riley was lying through his teeth.

"Did you get anything out of him?"

Riley shrugged, toed off his socks, and stripped off his boxers, until finally he stood naked by their bed. His hand immediately went to his dick, and he began running a hard grip from root to tip. It wasn't enough to get off, or even to get harder, but it was enough to make the light in Jack's eyes turn from concerned to completely confused. Life-affirming sex was what Riley wanted, and it was what he was going to get if he had his way.

He didn't say anything, just climbed onto the bed as provocatively as a six-foot-four man could and then reached into the drawer for lube. He looked over his shoulder.

"Coming?" He smirked when he saw Jack already had his pants off and was rapidly pulling everything else away.

"I need a shower." Jack looked hopefully toward the bathroom and wiped the sweat on his face with his shirt.

"No, you don't," Riley nearly growled. He just wanted Jack now. In him. Around him. Holding him.

"Jesus, Riley." Jack was fisting himself, and in a quick move, he had the bedroom door locked and was grabbing at the lube.

"I don't need much," Riley insisted.

"Shut the fuck up. I'm not hurting you." Jack smoothed the cool liquid over Riley. It wasn't soft or sensuous, though—it was claiming and marking and animalistic.

Riley held on to the headboard, gripping hard to the carved wood, fingers so tight that he felt one of the ornate posts give from the strain and loosen under his weight. He whimpered as Jack finished preparing him and pushed his way in.

Jack was fast and hard, and his fingers dug into Riley's hips. Every thrust forward was met by Riley pushing back, and Riley was going to be covered in bruises tomorrow.

"What... happened? Tell... me," Jack demanded with each push.

But Riley couldn't tell him yet. To grab his dick, he released one hand from the carved posts, his other arm taking the full strain of this cowboy fucking him into the mattress. He was so close. It didn't matter what was in his head; this was primal and now. The head of his dick was wet, and the friction between hand and pillow was getting him there.

Jack stiffened above him and the sound he made was nearly a howl as he reached his completion. The feel of Jack inside him and the pain of his short nails carving into Riley's skin was enough to send him into an orgasm so hard he saw black. Jack pulled out and fell back on the bed, and every muscle in Riley's body betrayed him. He collapsed where he was, right on top of the wet patch. And he really didn't give a shit.

"What happened today, Ri?" Jack asked between panted breaths.

Riley loved it when Jack shortened his name like that. So much affection and familiarity dripped from that single syllable. "I don't know. Jenkins looked like an accountant, and he told me this stuff about a guy in Martha's Vineyard, and then he received a text and left. I paid the bill."

"Were the Feds cool with what they got? Is it enough?"

It was a simple question. Riley answered it in his head just fine, but when he tried to form the sentence, the words were too far away for him to grab hold of.

"Ri?"

"Someone shot him."

The silence was dangerous, the calm before the storm.

"Who? Jenkins? Who shot him?"

"I don't know."

"When?"

"When I was paying the check."

"In the restaurant?"

"On the sidewalk." Riley didn't want to recall the blood or the spray of brain matter up the wall, but the image appeared instantly.

"You were inside the restaurant?" Jack was still deceptively calm.

Riley winced before turning his face to look right at him. "I was inside."

"What if you hadn't been, Riley? What if you'd walked out with him?"

"The shot was pretty much dead center." Riley indicated his forehead with a tap of a finger. "They knew who they were aiming for."

Jack closed his eyes, and in a single motion, he rolled to his feet and grabbed at his jeans. He began to get dressed, wearing a very determined expression.

"Jack, what are you doing?"

"I'm going to find Agent Jones," he spat. "And I'm going to kill him."

Riley's chest tightened; he pushed himself to stand between Jack and the door. "No. Don't rise to it."

"That... *suit*... put my husband in the line of fire. I. Will. Kill. Him."

Jack stopped centimeters from him, and Riley had never felt as vulnerable as he did being completely naked between Jack in a temper and the cold wood behind him.

"Jack. Stop. This isn't something you can solve with your fists."

"Don't patronize me."

"I'm not. Come on, Jack. It's over."

Jack stared at him mutinously. Then something snapped in him, and his eyes filled with worry. "Are you going to move out of my way?" he asked.

"No." Riley's tone brooked no discussion.

"I can take you."

"You can try."

"I am so fucking pissed, Ri."

"I know. I don't blame you. But please... Jack... we have Hayley to think about now."

Jack's shoulders relaxed, and little by little, the rest of his tense muscles loosened visibly. He closed both of his large hands around Riley's face. His grip was so tight, and the kiss that came with it was forceful. When Jack pulled away, Riley could taste blood.

"Never again." Jack wasn't asking for a discussion; he was demanding.

"Never again," Riley said.

CHAPTER 17

Living with a daughter had Riley doing things he'd thought he'd never do. With Jack's family, he had always been involved on the periphery of what the kids were up to, but to actually have to dress up for Halloween was a new one. He was Dracula, and the face paints left a mess on the covers when Jack—aka The Cowboy Who Had Risen from the Dead—made love to him in full makeup.

Riley had pointed out there was no such character as the one Jack had portrayed. Hayley, with a very serious expression on her face, had informed Riley that Halloween was *pretend*.

He didn't think he could love her more.

Thanksgiving was this huge family dinner, and Donna had chosen to hold the entire thing at the place where she was living—Neil's house at the veterinary practice. The combination kitchen-dining room was an old converted barn big enough for assorted family members to congregate. Older tables were pushed next to the large oak table in the center, and the whole thing was covered in red cloths. Donna was in her element, and she had Sandra on kitchen duty alongside her. Jim was playing super grandpa, and Neil and Josh spent a long time discussing sports. Eden had brought along her journalist. Riley was thankful big time, because it put a smile on Jack's face to have someone new to talk horses with.

Riley managed to corner his sister for a ten-minute chat. "Sean is sure making himself cozy," he started—and then cursed to himself because the words sounded a little off even to his own ears.

To her credit, Eden didn't rise to the big-brother baiting. "He's a good guy," she said instead and glanced over at her boyfriend fondly.

Riley followed her glance, but he was more interested in the animated expression on Jack's face. "Should I be worried?"

"What about?"

"About him and you and your money?" Riley winced again. Maybe he was being a little too 'in your face.'

"He knows how much money I have in the bank, Riley, but he fell in love with me for me."

"Are you sure?"

"How can we ever be sure?"

"Did you get Jim to run a background check on him?" Riley narrowed his eyes as he saw Jack throw back his head and laugh loudly.

"I did," Eden said. "We couldn't find him in police databases, but his fingerprints were with the FBI, the CIA, and Interpol. His two alien abductions are on record as well."

It took Riley a few seconds to realize his sister was teasing him. When he did, though, he cuffed her upside the head. She rubbed the area of impact with a muttered "*Ow*."

Riley continued. "Just… he seems like a nice guy, and Jack likes him. Is he…. Has he…. Jeez, are you two…?"

"What?" She leaned in to him with a conspiratorial whisper. "Doing the nasty?"

Riley pulled back in horror. "I meant are you serious about each other!" He really didn't want to think of his baby sister kissing, let alone sleeping with someone.

Eden just laughed. "Well, we haven't exchanged promise rings yet." She sniggered.

"Okay…." Now what did he say?

Thankfully she changed the subject, eliminating his desperate need to find something more to say.

"The article was good."

"Yes, it was," he agreed, relieved.

"And it's been received well."

"We got invited to *Ellen*," Riley said.

"Really? Are you going to do it?" she asked curiously.

"No freaking way." Riley and Jack had taken one look at each other when the call came through and said the same thing. "We think it may just settle down now."

Sean and Jack chose that moment to walk up to them, and Riley tried his hardest to be the kind, supportive brother as opposed to the leave-my-sister-alone version.

"Beth and Josh want a family chat," Jack said, and with a quick kiss to Riley's lips, he left.

Riley watched him go, caught between wanting to admire the man from the back and worrying about why Jack's siblings wanted a family chat.

This didn't bode well.

* * * * *

Jack found his brother and sister, their heads held close in conversation, outside in the yard. They moved apart quickly when he said hi, and he narrowed his eyes at the guilt in their expressions.

"I'm not going to like this, am I?" He sighed.

Josh and Beth exchanged glances.

"For the record," Josh began, "we know exactly what you're going to say, and we understand where you're coming from."

"Okay…" He took the proffered beer from Josh's hand and drank a third in two swallows. He might need the alcoholic support if his suspicions were correct and this was to do with his mom.

"Neil came to see me," Josh said. "He said that as the eldest—" He held up a hand to stop Jack speaking. "—he wanted to ask for my blessing because he's going to ask Mom to marry him. He wants you and Beth to do the same thing, so it's all of us."

Jack shifted uncomfortably under their expectant looks. Neil was a good guy, an excellent vet, and he'd done so much with Taylor. He was a career man with a large house, and it appeared he had money in the bank. Donna was smitten, and Neil was good to her, good with her. It was just the damn twenty-year age gap and the fact that Neil was young enough to be Jack's brother.

The thing was, Jack had taken on the responsibility of the D, and part of that was watching out for his mom. He hadn't gone off to college like Josh, and Beth often needed care and wasn't able to add her support as much as she wanted. Which just left Jack himself. Maybe he should try and explain he just needed time to adjust?

"Do you want to know what I think?" Beth interrupted his line of thinking in her quiet voice.

Jack looked at her expectantly. Beth was always the mediator, the calm one who made sense of things in their family when brotherly testosterone got in the way. Jack nodded, and Josh encouraged her with a "Go on."

"Emily loves him—" she started. Jack agreed his niece really did have a soft spot for the vet. "—and I really like him, and it makes me sad to see Momma alone. Most of all, I trust him."

"I agree with Beth," Josh said simply.

Jack looked from one to the other and felt his prejudice melt away under their acceptance of the guy in his mom's life. "Okay." He pushed his hands into his jeans pockets. "I guess he has my blessing as well."

When they walked back into the kitchen, Donna and Neil were in the middle of a flour fight, with a grinning Riley trying to break them apart. Jack couldn't help himself. The sight of his husband, in his customary black pants and shirt, covered in white handprints, with Donna laughing beside him was a great thing to see.

Jack listened, even as Neil looked over at the three of them with concern on his face. Josh must have indicated something because suddenly Neil grabbed Donna's hand and exited stage left to the pantry. The kitchen was chaotic with kids and laughter, teasing and food, and no one really noticed when the two came back to the table. Although Donna looked a little flushed and Neil had a grin as wide as the state, no one said a thing.

Once the turkey was carved and everyone had plates piled high with food, Neil raised his voice above the general chatter. "We have an announcement," he said clearly, and everyone stopped talking to listen.

Jack felt his stomach churn, and blindly reached for Riley's hand under the table. Riley gripped it hard. Jack sensed him looking, but he didn't meet Riley's gaze.

Neil stood and encouraged Donna to stand with him. Jack really didn't think he'd ever seen her looking so relaxed and happy, and as quickly as butter melted in the sun, his final doubts disappeared. Riley was tracing a pattern on his palm, and the regular movement was soothing; it grounded him.

"With Josh, Jack, and Beth's blessing, I have asked Donna to marry me." He looked down at her, and she smiled and leaned into his hold. Collectively, the whole family appeared to hold their breath. "She said yes."

The table erupted in cheers. Emily started to cry, and in an instant, Jack scooped her up before Beth could get to her. He shook hands with Neil, kissed his mom on the cheek, and hugged her one-armed. Then he sat, attempting to eat a full Thanksgiving dinner with a baby who'd fallen asleep on his chest.

CHAPTER 18

When Riley woke, it was to an eerie light through the cracks in the drawn drapes. He blearily extricated himself from Jack's grip to go to the bathroom, and after he'd washed his hands, he moved to the window.

He pulled the drapes. "Holy shit!" He couldn't hold back his curse.

Jack shot bolt upright in bed, staring madly, trying to find the reason for Riley's curse as well as its volume. He was fighting sheets one minute, and the next was at Riley's side, as naked as the day he was born, staring out of the window.

"*Holy shit.*" He repeated Riley's sentiment.

"Hayley—"

"Hayley—"

They said it at the same time, and in a flurry of movement, were dressed, teeth brushed, and their hair pushed back under caps from the back of Jack's closet.

Riley reached her room first and crossed straight to her bed. Falling to his knees by her side, he shook her gently.

Her tousled head appeared from way under the covers. "Wha…?" was her level of coherency, but as Jack pulled back her drapes and she blearily looked over, it was an instant wake-up call.

"Snow!" she shrieked and rolled out of the covers.

Together, they found clothes to wrap her up in. Riley insisted on four layers; Jack said three was enough. Hayley, desperate to get outside, just wanted a coat over her PJs.

When her boots were finally on, Riley pushed open the mudroom door against a heaped deposit of snow, and together, all three took their first steps into the untouched white world.

"Did you know it was going to snow?" Riley asked Jack, who always had an eye on weather news.

"Not at all. Jeez. It never snows here in December. Last year we got an inch in February, and it disappeared overnight. Remember?"

"Santa brought it for me," Hayley whispered conspiratorially and darted off as quickly as she could. "I need to see Red," she called over her shoulder.

They followed her at a slower pace, and Riley looked up at cloudless sky. "It's going to be gone by tomorrow, isn't it?"

"Most likely."

They watched from the gate as Hayley crossed to the barns and started chatting away to Red.

"Will the horses be okay in the barns?"

"I'll keep an eye out, but yes, they should be fine. Snow'll be gone by tomorrow, and we can turn them out."

"Wanna make a snowman?" Riley's question might have been tongue-in-cheek, but when Jack grinned like a kid, he felt a lightness in him he hadn't felt for weeks. "Hayley, want to build a snowman?"

"Coming." She ran back to them, her cheeks flushed, her eyes bright.

They built a snowman: not a particularly big one, but he looked cute and was nearly the same height as Hayley. They decorated him with stones and a carrot, and then made snow angels, lying there laughing like idiots, even though the cold was eating through Riley's jeans.

After going inside to get fresh clothes and coffee and hot chocolate, they took seats on the sheltered porch, and Riley's world was complete.

His cell vibrated in his pocket, and more out of habit than desire, he checked the caller.

"Hi, Dad." He smiled as he answered the call. "Like the snow?"

"I had some disturbing news, Riley."

Riley sat up, exchanging a worried glance with Jack.

Jim continued. "I received notification on the filed papers for a petition of custody from Sarah and Elliot Anderson. As we thought, it was rejected, but that isn't what's worrying me. The files are dated four days ago, and I just got off the phone with Sarah. Seems like Elliot isn't handling the news so well, had some kind of minor breakdown. He left two days ago, saying he'd get money one way or another. Sarah thought he was blowing off steam, but when he didn't come back last night and she checked the gun safe…."

"She thinks he's going to come here and he's armed," Riley finished for him.

"What's wrong?" Jack leaned forward, but Riley waved him back.

"I don't know. We could call the cops out on him, just in case. But if he's coming out to you to talk and we get the authorities involved and then it gets messy…. Why don't you just bring Hayley here or take her to Josh's for a while?"

"We'll go visit Josh." Riley ended the call and leaned back in his chair.

"Okay?" Jack asked.

"Hayley, why don't you go get dressed warmer, and we'll take you to visit Uncle Josh and your cousins."

"Yay!" She scrambled down from her seat and scampered into the house.

"Tell me, Riley."

"Elliot told Sarah he would be getting the money one way or another, and he left Abilene two days ago, with a gun."

"Shit, Ri. Do we need to call the cops?"

"Let's just get Hayley to Josh's. She can have a snow day with the kids. Then we'll come back and deal with a call to the police."

"You get Hayley situated, I'll check on Taylor and the foal, and we'll leave in ten, right?"

Jack stood in a flurry of motion, and in seconds he was off the porch and away to the barns and the paddocks behind them.

Riley didn't waste any time either. He got the gun cabinet open in seconds and pulled out a rifle and some rounds. If he needed to, he would meet a gun with a gun.

"Daddy?" Hayley didn't sound concerned. She clearly just wanted his attention. "Shall I take the cookies we made yesterday?"

Riley was speechless for a second. He needed to say something. Anything. But all he wanted to do was scoop her up, dump her in his SUV, grab Jack, and leave. It wasn't rational. Elliot was probably holed up somewhere with whiskey, nursing his failure to get money and going over all the what-ifs in his life. Why would he make his way to the D? What could he gain from facing down Riley and Jack with a gun?

"Sorry, baby?" He'd forgotten what she wanted.

"The cookies I made with Grandma Donna. Should we take them?"

"Good idea, sweetheart. Get your bag and we'll grab them on the way through."

In five minutes, they were in Riley's car, and he had the engine ticking over, warming the inside and letting the heat clear some of the snow. It was slow going. Riley checked the time. Jack was taking too long with the horses. They needed to get Hayley over to Josh's as soon as they could. He didn't want her here with a freaking madman on the loose. He tapped his fingers in a rhythm on the steering wheel. *Come on, come on.*

He glanced to the left toward the barns. Jack was nowhere to be seen.

"Daddy!" Hayley's shriek of fear sent ice down Riley's spine and he spun in his seat. The loaded rifle was just out of reach.

He recognized Elliot immediately. The man stood right in front of the car, holding a snub-nosed revolver and aiming it straight at Hayley. Not him… Hayley. The gun didn't waver. Elliot's expression was set in stone, and it was clear what he wanted.

The front of Elliot's coat was covered in blood, and there was more on his face.

Shit. Is that Jack's blood?

Riley was transfixed, utterly unable to think of what to do and where to turn. Was Jack injured somewhere? How was he going to get Hayley away from this man? Should he drive away? Leave Jack—Shit, there was so much blood on Elliot, but Jack would want him to take Hayley and drive the fuck away from the D. If anything happened to Hayley, Jack would hate him for staying.

"You want me to go back and finish him?" Elliot shouted through the window.

Relief flooded through Riley. So Jack wasn't dead, but he was lying injured somewhere. His knuckles whitened on the steering wheel. Elliot was nearly a foot shorter than Riley. It would be easy to use some of that extra body weight to take the guy out. What if he floored the pedal and ran the guy down? The gun was still pointing at Hayley, though, and Riley wasn't going to risk her life.

He wasn't left with any real choices.

"I'm giving you until the count of five, Hayes."

CHAPTER 19

"Five."

Riley went through options for a way out of this. None of them made any sense. He glanced over his shoulder, contemplating driving through the gate in reverse and getting Jack in the car and both of them away before Elliot got a shot in.

It wasn't going to happen.

"Four."

"*Hayley*," Riley said loud enough that she could hear over her sobs. "I'm getting out of the car, and I want you to stay in here."

"No, Daddy." She gripped his arm tight, and the number three echoed into the car as Elliot kept counting.

"Hayley, I need you to do this for me. As soon as I leave the car, you press the button to lock the doors again. Can you see it? The car symbol?"

"Daddy—"

"Can you see it, Hayley?"

"I can."

"Two. Hayes, get out of the car."

"Lock the doors and stay inside… whatever happens."

"Daddy?"

"Will you do that for me, baby?"

"I will, but, D-daddy, don't die—"

Riley looked direct into her brown eyes swimming in tears, and he saw the naked fear within them. He pasted his best reassuring smile on his face. "I won't die, Hayley. I promise you. I love you. Pappa loves you too."

"One, Hayes."

In a smooth move, Riley was out of the car, his feet on the ground and the door shut behind him. He heard the *snick* of the locks. At least for now, his daughter was safe.

"What the hell, Elliot?" he said brusquely. Putting Elliot on the defensive could possibly be a good move— but it might also be a bad one. "You're not taking Hayley."

"I don't want *Hayley*."

Elliot laughed sharply, the abrupt noise dripping with madness. He appeared momentarily unfocused, and for an instant, Riley wondered whether perhaps the man had left prison with one too many habits he couldn't break.

"I just want money. You have money." Elliot displayed the absolute logic of a man on the edge. "Sarah won't go for taking Hayley, so I'm comin' directly to the bank, so to speak."

"I don't have money here." Riley injected as much calm as he could into his voice while, inside, his heart was nearly beating out of his chest. Elliot was two paces away—not close enough for Riley to make an attempt to grab at the gun.

Considering his glassy-eyed disorientation, Elliot remained lucid enough to hold the weapon with an absolute, solidly horizontal aim. "Do I look stupid?"

When Riley didn't answer, Elliot repeated himself. "Do. I. Look. Fucking. Stupid?"

The gun wavered a bit, and Riley retreated until his back was against the car door. "No."

"I have an account. I want you to transfer over what I need."

Relief flooded through Riley. He could do that. He moved and felt the weight of his cell in his pocket. Shit. He should have given it to Hayley. God, did she even know how to use a cell?

"Get into the house."

Elliot's harsh voice broke into his thoughts and Riley snapped back to see him gesturing with the gun, indicating Riley should go first. As he turned to go around the car, he caught sight of Hayley's face, her eyes wide with fear. Fuck. If he got his hands around Elliot's neck, he would surely squeeze the life out of him for scaring her like this.

He would kill him.

* * * * *

Sitting at the computer with a gun to his head made it nearly impossible for Riley to concentrate. From where they sat, in the small office next to their bedroom, Riley could see where he and Jack had slept only hours before. The bedclothes were still awry from their excitement that morning, and Riley focused on that, his fingers hesitating over the keys.

A slip of paper dropped onto the desk, and the feel of cold hard steel at his temple pulled him back to the here and now.

"Nice little offshore encrypted transfer from you, Mr. Hayes."

"*Six million?*" Riley read from the paper. "Where do you think I'm going to find that kind of—?"

The barrel of the gun pressed harder.

"It's pocket change for you. A whole new life for me.

Fucking find it."

Riley racked his brains. Any ready cash he had was tied up with Hayley now, and all he could recall was one personal account and another set up for CH Consultancy. He had no idea how much was in either, and not for the first time, he cursed the ignorance that only a very rich man could ever suffer from, as well as his own idiocy. The screen confirmed the first account held $2.4 million, and he transferred the entire balance to the bank indicated on the note. The CH Consultancy account held just over $1 million.

"It's all I can get hold of in such a short amount of time." Just shy of $3.5 million.

Elliot barked a laugh. "Poor little rich boy," he singsonged. He moved back, away from Riley, extending his arm with the gun still fixed on Riley's head. "It'll have to do."

Riley's finger hovered over the Enter key. When he pressed it, would Elliot shoot him?

"Press the freaking key," Elliot ordered. He gestured with the gun. "Or I'll do it for you when you're dead." Expecting to die the very next minute, Riley did as he was told and the confirmation of the transaction appeared on the screen.

No bullet tore through his head, and he looked up at Elliot, wishing his life would flash before his eyes but instead experiencing fear so thick it hurt. Some of the madness had dissipated from Elliot's eyes; Riley's assailant appeared calm and icily dispassionate.

"Get up and go into your bedroom," he ordered.

At the point of the gun, Riley stood and moved to the

adjoining room. If he had to die, he wished it wasn't going to be in the room that held so much evidence of his life with Jack in the clothes scattered around the room, the jeans over the end of the bed, the half-empty bottle of water on Jack's nightstand.

He tried to reach the heart of the man with the gun. "Killing me will destroy Hayley."

Elliot tossed him some heavy-duty cuffs. Hard and unyielding, they felt cold in his hands.

"Cuff yourself to the bed."

Riley closed the cuff around one hand and, inspired, wrapped the chain around the third carved post from the right. He finished off by snapping the other side shut. He was a prisoner.

"I'm not a killer, Hayes," Elliot said simply. "I like Hayley, always have. Your money is well hidden now, perks of being a hacker. People underestimate an ex-con, but a few keystrokes and Elliot Anderson becomes someone else, a ghost no one can find." He reached forward to grab at something lying nearby. With a barked laugh, he lifted the items to look at them closer and then pocketed them. "*Two* Rolexes? Who the fuck needs two Rolexes?"

And with that, he left.

Riley counted to ten and then used his body weight to pull at the loose post. It hadn't fitted properly since their hard coming together after Riley saw Jenkins shot dead on the street. Soon free, he went immediately to the gun cabinet.

Being armed in the house was his first priority, calling for help his second. He reported the incident in hushed tones and replaced the handset as soon as he was convinced the dispatcher understood the importance.

Feeling safer armed, he moved out to the front of the house, taking each corner as he'd seen cops in the movies do, with the gun held out in front of him. The house was devoid of life apart from himself. He wondered which way Elliot had left. There had been no sign of a car or any other vehicle he may have used to get to the D ranch house. He must have used the old stock road to the rear of the barns, out of sight of the house.

Hayley was still in the car, her knees pulled up and her arms wrapped around them. She looked scared and forlorn.

Riley smiled and nodded at her. He indicated with a hand that she should stay where she was, and she nodded her understanding. His beautiful, brave daughter. He crossed to the car very slowly, still very aware of what was happening around them, and when he reached her side, she unlocked the door.

"Daddy?"

"I'm okay, sweetheart. Stay here for the police and keep the door locked. Okay?"

"Where's Pappa?"

"I'm going to get him, baby. Lock the door." He pushed it closed as quietly as he could but winced at the sound of metal on metal as it shut.

Hayley did as he asked, locking the doors and staring out at him. After he blew her a kiss, he made his way cautiously around the edge of the house to the back barns. There he spotted what Jack had probably seen: tire marks in the snow away from the old barn. Riley could imagine only too well Jack going over to the vehicle, wondering why the hell it was on his land. There was no vehicle there now, but Riley wasn't ready to accept that Elliot had truly left.

The first blood he saw was outside their barn. *Their* barn. God. Riley wanted to shout, but he couldn't chance Elliot being still around with a new manic expression and his loaded gun. The snow was a mess of red and mud, and it looked like someone had been dragged inside the barn.

He walked in as quietly as he could and strained to hear any noise. Nothing. Then he spotted Jack, a crumpled heap on the blankets in the corner, and with a muffled cry, unmindful of who the hell else could be there, he dropped to his knees next to the figure of his prone husband.

Blood. There was so much blood, and Riley struggled to turn him over. He checked for bullet wounds, but could find nothing apart from an impressive gash across Jack's head. That seemed to be the reason for all the blood.

"Jack." He shook him hard enough to wake the dead, and with a groan, Jack's eyelids fluttered. "Come on, Jack… wake up."

Shocked blue eyes looked up at him. "Wha' happened?"

"Elliot happened."

"Hayley?"

"She's fine. Stay here. I'll be back."

After scrambling to stand, he retraced his steps to the car and opened the door, holding out a hand. When Hayley grasped it, he pulled her into a tight hug. She buried her face in his neck, and with no further thought, he stalked back to Jack. The cold of the snow was suddenly very obvious. He shivered, but it was half from cold and half from adrenaline overload.

Once back with Jack, he slumped down with a stall wall at his rear and slid until Jack's head was in his lap. Hayley was still gripping his arm to his other side. He took his cell from Hayley's hand.

"Is Pappa going to be okay?"

"I'm fine, Hayley."

Jack's voice was more growl than substance, but at least he was conscious.

Riley thumbed through his recent calls, found the contact he wanted, and it connected almost immediately.

"Jones."

"My daughter's uncle threatened us with a gun, hit my husband across the head, threatened my daughter, and stole over $3 million to an offshore account. Cops are on their way. Thing is, Agent Jones, I don't know how your alien tech works, but he took the watch."

Call finished, Riley pulled at the blankets until Hayley was covered and lying with Jack. Riley sat with the gun pointing forward, and he didn't move until the cops arrived.

Not one single muscle.

* * * * *

Elliot was tracked heading north on US 75 and subsequently captured. When Agent Jones told Riley, he had to bite back the need to find out where they were holding Elliot just so he could go and beat the shit out of him.

The entire family descended on them, snow or no snow.

After everyone left, the adrenaline finally faded from Riley's body and left him in something akin to shock.

Jack was up and walking; the doc had given him a fairly clean bill of health but with the usual warnings. The blow to the head and the blood loss were more scary than life-threatening, despite the short lack of consciousness, and he'd refused to go to the hospital.

Selfishly, Riley was more than happy with that decision, and he promised he would watch over Jack at home for any signs of concussion.

Once Hayley was asleep, all Riley wanted to do was hold Jack. He shuffled to one side of the bed, pulled him close in a hug, and then cradled him against his chest.

"Hayley seems okay," Jack said so quietly that Riley had to strain to hear.

"She said she never liked Elliot." He sighed. It never failed to amaze him how perceptive kids could be. "In her eyes, he was already the bad guy. All he did was cement that fact, and she wasn't surprised."

"Poor kid."

"Jesus, Jack—" Riley's grip tightened in Jack's hair, and Jack made a muffled protest. "—we didn't know what had happened to you," he repeated for about the hundredth time. "Elliot was covered in your blood."

"He hit me near his truck. Guess the blood came from him dragging me into the barn."

"Don't do that again." Riley pressed a kiss to his shower-damp hair.

"What?" Jack chuckled. "Get myself hit in the head with a hunk of two-by-four?"

"Yeah, that."

"I'll try not to."

"Daddy?"

Riley looked up. Hayley stood in the doorway, her stuffed dog in one hand and the other curled into her PJ top. Wordlessly the two men separated from their hug, making a Hayley-sized space between them. She climbed in, leaned into Jack, and clung to him briefly. Then she did the same to Riley.

No one said anything, and in a few minutes, she was curled into a tight ball, her breathing low and even. Tears choked Riley's throat, and he looked at Jack, who appeared just as affected. This scrap of humanity, his daughter, was possibly the best thing to happen to them next to meeting each other.

"I love you," he whispered to his husband over Hayley's sleeping form.

"Love you," Jack replied.

On the pillow above her head, in front of a broken carved post, they held hands.

EPILOGUE

There was no snow on Christmas Day. There never really was in Texas, and neither Riley nor Jack had expected it.

The whole family descended on the D, and despite Donna cooking dinner, to Riley it felt like they were hosting Christmas in their own house.

Donna announced her and Neil's wedding was set for Valentine's Day. Eden and Sean looked way past friendly, and Sean's proposal over the main course wasn't entirely unexpected. Beth and Steve passed on the news that Beth's last rounds of tests were good and the doctors had deemed her heart stronger. Sandra and Jim watched, smiling and holding hands.

The conversation turned to the FBI and the forged documents that had caused Riley to need to do what he could to make things right.

"And you still don't know what the Feds wanted in all of this?"

"Apart from names further up the food chain? No. They set me up. They set that accountant up."

"They never said one word about... y'know?" Eden asked curiously with a wave of her hand.

They weren't talking about things in front of the kids. No sense in blurting out the whole mess in explicit detail.

"Nothing." Riley shrugged and went back to concentrating on his meal, with the reassuring warmth of Jack's arm pressed close to his.

"Are you going to get your money back from that

transfer you did?" Jim asked at a break in the conversation.

Riley looked at his dad. The money had never been an issue, not after nearly losing Jack and with Hayley in danger. Sometimes he wondered if having money was something that always brought unhappiness, or whether he'd just been unlucky.

When the FBI had contacted him to say the account had been found and the transfer reversed, he realized he didn't care. Familiar anxiety built in him.

As if sensing Riley's confusion, Jack leaned in to him and hand-fed him a carrot, and the butter slid along his lip. A subtle lick of Jack's fingers and the reassurance in his husband's blue eyes was enough to center him.

"The FBI released the funds to the bank. It's all there, apparently," he finally said.

Steve smirked. "Drinks on you next time we're out, then." He leaned down from his chair to swing Emily up onto his lap.

It seemed like yesterday that she was a baby in Beth's arms, and now, here she was walking and falling over a lot. Riley and Jack had bought her a toy keyboard, and Steve had threatened to kill them or buy Hayley a drum kit—whichever was the worse revenge for the discordant noise Emily could now create.

It was perfect: chaotic and noisy but brimming with love. Each person at the table received a small gift from under the tree, deliberately left away from the huge piles of gifts the kids had opened. Nothing expensive, the gifts ranged from books to DVDs to a pair of SpongeBob socks for Jim.

Hayley had a joint present for her two dads, and she handed it to them with a smile of unlimited joy. "I made it," she said. "Though Aunty Eden helped."

Jack inclined his head to indicate Riley should open the box, so he did. Inside was the most intricate tree ornament dripping with silver and red sparkles.

Riley held it up, and it spun on its short string, the light from overhead twinkling in the mirrored, sprinkled glitter. He stopped the spin and focused in on the tiny photos he recognized from their interview, little thumbnails of him and Jack and Hayley. She'd glued them in a group along with a handwritten label.

Daddy, Pappa, and me.
My family.

THE END

Made in the USA
San Bernardino, CA
22 March 2018